"I know I shouldn't have walked into your house and started cleaning, but I knocked and you didn't answer. I just meant to straighten up a little but I got carried away."

He just cocked his head to the side and looked at her.

"I was feeling restless," she explained.

"I can tell." He took off his gloves, tossed them onto the counter and came toward her. "You just can't come into a man's home and be bent over in his refrigerator without some consequences."

"Consequences?" She swallowed hard. "How about a thank-you, you big jerk? Your house is a disaster and I've been working my fingers to the bone to make it habitable."

"Oh, poor princess. Had to do some actual work and now she's all worn-out." He placed his big hot hands around her waist and she couldn't think clearly.

"Shut up, Derek."

"Okay." He placed his mouth over hers and gave her a shockingly sexual kiss, and what was even more shocking was that she let him. She wrapped her arms around him and kissed him back. It wasn't something she could control anymore.

Dear Reader,

In *Mine at Midnight*, you'll meet Ava and Derek, two strong-willed people who want nothing to do with each other or falling in love. Join them on beautiful Hideaway as they figure out who they are and discover that they can't live without each other.

*Jamie*

# MINE AT MIDNIGHT

## Jamie Pope

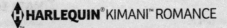

HARLEQUIN® KIMANI™ ROMANCE

Recycling programs
for this product may
not exist in your area.

33614080169997

ISBN-13: 978-0-373-86490-4

Mine at Midnight

Printed in U.S.A.

**Jamie Pope** first fell in love with romance when her mother placed a novel in her hands at the age of thirteen. She became addicted to love stories and has been writing them ever since. When she's not writing her next book, you can find her shopping for shoes or binge watching shows on Netflix.

## Books by Jamie Pope

### Harlequin Kimani Romance

*Surrender at Sunset*
*Love and a Latte*
*A Vow of Seduction* (with Nana Malone)
*Kissed by Christmas*
*Mine at Midnight*

To Jason,
I'm dedicating this book to you just because I like you.

# Chapter 1

Ava Bradley wasn't often nervous. Her twin brother often said that she had cold water running through her veins, that she was an ice princess. But today, as she stood in the living room of her charming seaside cottage, she felt anything but cold. Her heart was racing. Pounding so hard she wondered if it was going to burst out of her chest.

An enormous black garment bag had just been hand delivered to her by the designer after more than a thousand hours of work had been put into what was inside.

It was his masterpiece, as he called it.

Ava called it her wedding dress.

Her $25,000, crystal-encrusted, frothy confection of a wedding gown.

Most brides would be nervous, excited to receive their completed gowns.

It symbolized closing the door completely on one life and starting another.

But Ava didn't feel excitement. She felt more like throwing up.

This was her second wedding gown. She had purchased a simple but elegant one originally, which she had found in a shop right on Hideaway Island. It had been love at first sight. The ivory gown was vintage inspired, something a young bride might have worn in the 1940s, but that wasn't the dress she was going to wear when she walked down the aisle.

Her fiancé wanted her to wear something...better, he called it. Something luxurious and extravagant. It seemed like such an incredible amount of money. They could feed Miami's homeless for years with that amount of cash, but her fiancé wanted her to have it, so she had it. It was like that with everything. The car she drove had to be top of the line. The handbag she carried had to be so exclusive that most people were on a waiting list for a year just to be able to buy it. He was extremely wealthy and powerful, and he wanted his woman to reflect that.

"I only want the best, sweetheart," he purred in his Belgian accent. "That's why I picked you."

No, simple wouldn't do for Maxime Vermeulen. He was forty-four years old. Never married. He told her that he planned to be married only once, and that's why this wedding had to be the event of the century. Every time she had voiced her concerns about how much money they were spending, he would tell her that he had to spend it because she was perfect for him. And that she was beautiful and smart and lovely and all the things every woman wanted to hear from the man she was going to spend the rest of her life with.

*A perfect wedding, for my perfect bride.*

Ava had agreed to all of the pomp and circumstance to make him happy, although she had grown up in a working-class family in Maryland. Her father worked in a factory.

Her mother had worked two jobs when things were tight. Yes, her older brother had made it big in the major league, but never in a million years did Ava dream that she would land someone like Max. Someone who had always had so much and had no idea what it was like to fly in a plane that he didn't own. She'd met him by chance while she was working. She'd been a buyer for an exclusive chain of boutiques and had literally bumped into him walking out of a meeting. He'd dazzled her with his easy charm and devastating good looks.

He was good to her. He spoiled her silly and proudly showed her off to his friends. It was why she made sacrifices for him.

Small ones like quitting her job. And giving up her home and a tiny bit of her freedom. Max insisted that the wives of rich men didn't have jobs. He told her that he would look like a fool if he let her continue to live in her modest townhome instead of a penthouse apartment in an exclusive section of Miami. And the thought of her grocery shopping or even doing something as simple as making their bed nearly sent him into a series of fits.

*We have people to do that for us, my sweet.*

She didn't want to make Max look foolish. But she wasn't adjusting to the lifestyle of the rich and idle too well.

That's why she had thrown herself into planning the perfect wedding. There had been no planner or assistant. It didn't make sense for them to hire someone to do it when she could. Max indulged her on this. He thought it was because she was very particular, but the truth was she needed to plan this wedding because without her career she was bored.

And now the ceremony was upon them. Five more days. Guests were coming in from all over the world. Heads of state, members of royal families, politicians. These were the people they needed to impress. That's why Max insisted on the cake being made in the most exclusive bakery in New York and flown in the next day. He wanted flowers that were grown in special hothouses. A string quartet was being flown in from Belgium. And a celebrity chef and his crew of fifty were arriving to feed the hundreds of guests that were going to be present. There were so many moving parts, so many things that needed to be done on a deadline that it felt more like a job than the most meaningful day of her life. Maybe it was better that this felt like work, because the longer she focused on the work, the less time she had to think.

Think about him and their future and how she would be spending her time as his wife.

She hadn't seen Max at all this week. In fact, she had seen him only twice in the last thirty days. He traveled a lot for work, and they agreed to spend the days leading up to the wedding apart so that their honeymoon would be more special. Ava was hoping that he would slow down once they walked down the aisle. He had promised her that he would. That they would put down roots. Unfortunately, it couldn't be on this island, even though she had loved it since her parents had first taken her here as a little girl.

Maxime was a restaurateur, and she had convinced him to open up a small bistro on the island and staff it with local people. Their idea to open an oceanfront eatery had somehow expanded into a plan to build a massive resort. But the residents of the island, led by the mayor, made it impossible for him to even purchase land. Maxime had been furious. He wasn't a man that was used to hearing no. Ava had secretly been glad the plan had failed. A huge hotel would have taken away from the quaint, homey feeling of Hideaway Island, and that's what Ava loved about this place. Miami was good for nightlife and culture, but this place felt like home.

Maxime wanted nothing to do with it now. He had

wanted her to move the wedding off the island, but she had refused. She would quit her job to make him happy, plan a wedding that would rival all weddings, but she was going to get married on Hideaway Island. In the place her family spent summer vacations. In the oceanfront home her father had helped her older brother pick out before he passed away. She had grown up in Maryland, but this was the place where she felt closest to her father. She remembered him being so happy here. And as she walked down the aisle toward Maxime on her brother's arm, she would picture her father's smiling face.

Max wanted her to have a baby soon, but she wanted to wait a little while. She knew she couldn't hold him off much longer because he was older than she was, and he wanted to be an active father. Children and family were extremely important to him.

*I want to have as many as possible. My children are my legacy.*

She wanted children, too, but she wanted to spend some time with just him first. He was away so much that there were times when she felt like she barely knew him at all.

She tried to shake off the uneasy feelings that snuck into her chest and nearly suffocated her. She had been with him for more than three years. Of course she knew him. And if she didn't, she would have the rest of her life to get to know him.

Ava took a deep breath and finally unzipped the large garment bag that held her dress. She didn't even have to unzip it all the way to see the sparkle from all the hand-sewn crystals. Even if it wasn't exactly her taste, she had to admit it was magnificent. All that effort for something that she would wear for only a few hours. She wondered what her father would think of all this. He had been a simple man. She wondered if he would be impressed by it all or think it was crazy to spend this much. Deep down she knew the answer.

She hated to think that her father might be disappointed in the way she was leading her life, but she knew that he had just wanted her to be happy. In the end, Ava was happy when Maxime was happy.

A knock on the door distracted her from her musings. She thought it might be her sister in-law, Virginia, bringing her six-month-old by for a visit. Ava would happily quit wedding planning for an hour or two to spend time with her niece. She had been there when Virginia had given birth and for every little milestone that Bria had met. She loved being so near the next generation of her family and seeing her oldest brother, Carlos, being a father.

She zipped the garment bag up and headed to the front door. Only she didn't see her sister-in-law with her adorable little baby standing there. There was a woman that she'd never seen before. She was older, probably nearing forty, with plain brown hair and nondescript features. Ava had never had a visitor outside of her family and the delivery people since she'd been there.

"I don't mean to be rude," she started, "but I am very happy with my current faith at the moment."

"Oh, I'm not here for that reason, Ava."

She knew her name?

"You are Ava, aren't you? I recognize you from your pictures."

Maxime wasn't quite a celebrity, but because of his massive business holdings and his family's last name on a string of luxury hotels he was well known and sometimes his picture was snapped by the paparazzi. She was sure she had been photographed with him a few times, but that didn't explain why the woman was there.

"How can I help you?" Ava tried not to let her nervousness show. There was a strange woman at her rental home, and she was alone. She had taken some self-defense classes, but right now that information had flown out of her head while other more troubling thoughts had crashed around into it.

"I'm Ingrid."

She studied Ava's face for some kind of reaction.

"You don't know who I am, do you? Max never told you," she said sounding disappointed.

"Told me what?" Her stomach dropped. Sick was the only way she could describe how she was feeling.

"I think it might be better for me to show you rather than tell you. May I come in? You're probably going to need to sit down."

"I don't want to sit down, and I don't want to go inside. I want you to tell me why you are here."

Ingrid pulled a small photo album out of her oversize handbag and handed it to Ava. Ava opened it slowly. The first picture was of Maxime with a newborn swaddled in a blue blanket in his arms. His eyes were adoring. She had never seen that look in them before.

"That was nearly sixteen years ago now," Ingrid said softly.

Ava flipped to the next page to see a younger Ingrid with two small children, a boy and a girl, her head thrown back in laughter. Max sat next to her, a grin on his face and love in his eyes.

Ava wanted to ask if Ingrid was his long-lost sister, if those two children were his niece and nephew, but she already knew the answer. And yet she kept turning the pages. There was Ingrid with yet another baby, in a hospital bed, Max's arm wrapped around her. Ava walked back inside then and sat down heavily on her couch. She couldn't think. She just couldn't muster one coherent thought. But she kept turning those pages. Family vacations and birthday parties. Smiling faces. Happy times. She had hoped that this was a past relationship, but as she turned the pages she could see that Max was still very much a part of their lives. It was clear that when he wasn't with her, he was with them. He had the kind of life with them that she hoped they would have together.

She was more than stunned, more than shocked. She was paralyzed as she sat there.

"Our eldest is going to be sixteen in a few months. His name is Hugo. My middle's name is—"

"I don't want to know their names!" Ava pushed the photo album back at Ingrid, who had followed her inside. They were supposed to get married, spend the rest of their lives together. There were hundreds of people coming, some of them already there, and yet she was sitting next to the woman the man she loved had made a family with.

It was all going to waste. All the money that was spent that could have helped people. All the time she spent loving him, her career, it was all gone. Sacrificed for him.

"I'm not here to hurt you. I just thought you should know before you walked down the aisle that you would be sharing him with us. He said he was going to tell you. I had hoped he would tell you before you were married…"

"I don't understand." Ava shook her head. "Why are you a secret?"

"Look at me." She shrugged.

"What are you talking about? There is nothing wrong with the way you look."

Ingrid smiled at her. "He's right. You are sweet. I didn't think you would be from your pictures. I'm plain. I'm uninteresting. Uneducated. I was working as a waitress when we met. I always knew when I took up with him that I was never going to be the main woman in his life. He needs someone like you. Someone beautiful and graceful. You look like the wife of a billionaire. Plus he really does love you."

Ingrid had said so many things that Ava was having a hard time focusing on just one of them.

"How do you know he loves me?"

"He told me. We talk about you. He tells me everything. Max is my best friend."

"He doesn't tell me everything. I've spent three years with the man, and he couldn't be bothered to tell me that he was leading a double life."

"He was wrong for that. He should have told you from the beginning. I didn't want you to start your marriage off that way, and I didn't want you to find out by accident. But now that things are out in the open, you can discuss it with him and get past it."

"Get past it? There is nothing to get past. There's not going to be a marriage."

"Oh no!" Ingrid looked truly dismayed. "That wasn't my intention. You have to marry Max. He adores you. He's waited so long to get married. You're perfect for him."

"Do you think I'm the type of woman who would lower myself that far for a man?" Maybe it wasn't such a stretch, Ava had already given up a lot to be with him—what was the rest of her self-respect?

"Maxime isn't just any man. He's special and powerful, and millions of women would give up their souls to be where we are. He's so kind to me, and I know he's kind to you. There's no one else in the world who's going to give you what he can."

"I don't want what he can give me. And I'm sure as hell not willing to give up my soul to be with him." She stood up and walked to the door. "Now if you'll excuse me, I've got a wedding to cancel."

## Chapter 2

There was something big going on next door, Derek Patrick thought as he walked over to his window. He was a busy guy and usually nothing could tear him away from his work of making custom furniture and being the mayor of Hideaway Island, but the words "I'm going to kill the slimy bastard" had punctured his career-related fog.

Ava Bradley was staying next door to him. He hadn't realized it at first, because for the last week all he had seen were delivery trucks going in and out of her tiny driveway, but it certainly was her. Sister to his island's richest resident. Future wife of the man who'd tried to destroy Hideaway Island with a disgustingly large resort. As mayor Derek had done everything in his power to rally the citizens and prevent that. This place wasn't a resort town. It was an island full of hardworking people who wanted to live in peace. A resort of that size would have brought thousands of tourists in the summer. And he might've been okay with that if the billionaire was going to hire local people to build the monstrosity and to be lifeguards or housekeepers or whatever positions they had available, but that had never been an option. Vermeulen had planned to bring in foreign workers from overseas and pay them a rate that no one could live on. It was damn near evil. Derek had gone toe to toe with the man. And almost came to blows with him.

He had won, which infuriated the Belgium businessman. That's why Derek was surprised to find out that Ava had rented the house next door. She clearly hadn't known that he would be living beside her. She probably would have strapped on her four-inch designer stilettos and hightailed it back to Miami. But she decided that she was going to throw the world's largest wedding right here on the island. He wasn't exactly sure why she chose this place.

She was one of those women who was too beautiful. Almost painfully so. She had perfectly smooth brown skin, and midnight-black hair that was always perfectly styled. Her clothes were ultraexpensive, and fit to her thin body like a glove. He never saw her without diamonds in her ears, he never saw her in flip-flops or flat shoes like most people in a beach community wore. He never saw her smile warmly or look happy, for that matter. He mostly saw her as eye candy, hanging on that rich man's arm. Nothing more than another expensive accessory.

She didn't fit in here, and yet he couldn't be mad at her for wanting to get married on the island. Even she had to see that Hideaway Island was one of the most beautiful places on the planet.

Some of her many, many guests had arrived early, filling up all the little inns, bed-and-breakfasts and boutique hotels on the island. They ate in the restaurants and shopped in the stores. A few of them had even stopped into his showroom in town and purchased some pieces. It was a nice little boost for their economy. The island wasn't antitourist.

No, They welcomed all people. They just didn't want some big corporate enterprise sucking the life out of this place.

Derek saw Ava's twin, Dr. Elias Bradley, get out of his car. He knew when he saw Elias's face that something bad had gone down.

"Where the hell is he?" he shouted. The doctor appeared more like a football player than a surgeon as he stalked toward the cottage.

Carlos, her older brother, came out of the house, the former baseball player looking even more furious, if that were possible. "I don't know, but when I find him. I'm going to kill him. I'm going to smash his head in."

Carlos's wife, Virginia, came out after him, holding their daughter. "Would you two hush?" She scolded. "This isn't what Ava needs right now, and you're scaring Bria."

"Give me my baby girl." Carlos's voice softened as he took his daughter in his arms and cuddled her. "Don't worry, sweetheart. Your daddy and uncle aren't going to kill that slimy bastard today. We don't know where he is. You don't have to worry, but he should."

Derek knew he should step away from the window. Being in his neighbor's business was not his style, but he couldn't make himself move. The whole town was buzzing about this wedding. And it all seemed to be falling apart before his eyes.

Ava stepped out of the house then. She hadn't said a word, but Derek's eyes went to her as soon as she stepped over the threshold. She was wearing one of those tight pencil skirts and a white blouse that gently flowed over her figure. She was an absolute knockout by any man's standards, but it was her face that caught Derek's attention. There were no tears, no blurry eyes from what he could see. Her expression was blank, nearly emotionless, one might see her and think she was cold, but she took her niece from her brother and brought the little girl close to her, squeezing her as she closed her eyes. And just before she did, Derek saw misery there, pure, uncovered misery. It was one of those haunting looks, made even worse by the fact that it had come from one of the most beautiful women that he had ever seen.

He felt sorry for her then. He didn't want to because he didn't like her. He didn't like the way she walked or spoke or dressed. He didn't like how she let herself be used as some rich man's accessory. She reminded him of his mother. An incredibly beautiful failed dancer turned social climber, whose self-worth came from being the woman of a rich man.

He learned from a lifetime of living with her that women like that didn't change. Derek stepped away from the window and back to his work space. It wasn't his business what caused that hurt look to take over Ava's face. She would find another man. She would be all right. Women like her always managed to make it somehow.

Ava sat alone in her rented cottage that night. Carlos, Virginia and Elias had left a few minutes ago after staying with her all day. It was nice to have her family rally around her. Having two large, protective brothers threatening to tear Max limb from limb made her feel surprisingly better.

And her sister-in-law was a godsend. "You want this wedding canceled. We'll get this wedding canceled." As an interior designer, Virginia was used to managing large projects and calling dozens and dozens of vendors was no small feat. But she had done it all with a baby on her hip. If Ava hadn't been so numb, she would have been amazed by her.

She could barely focus on anything; she just leaned against her twin brother, his strong body keeping her upright when she would have slumped. She and Elias usually fought like it was going out of style, but he was her twin. They had gone to college together and lived next door to each other and didn't let more than a day pass without speaking to each other. Carlos was like a father figure to her, but Elias was like a piece of her soul. She would have fallen apart if he hadn't ended his shift at the hospital early to get to her.

But she had sent them all away. Elias's job as a trauma surgeon was too important for him to be away, and Carlos and Virginia needed to put their little girl to bed. And so she was truly left alone with her thoughts again.

What the hell was she going to do with her life now? She had no job. She was sure she could get her old one back, and if not, she could find one someplace else. Maybe in New York or LA, but that thought didn't appeal to her. She didn't want to be that far away from her family. The thought of returning to Miami also made her sick. She had so many memories of Max there. So many places where he had wined and dined her all while keeping the fact that he had three children and another woman a secret from her.

He had businesses there. She was bound to run into him over and over again, which was dangerous, because in her current mood she wasn't sure if she could prevent herself from running over him.

Her cell phone rang, and for a moment she was tempted to ignore it, but it was probably her mother who spent most of her year in Costa Rica now that she was a widow. She hadn't been home when she had called the first time, and she didn't want to leave the news in a message. It just wasn't the kind of thing you said into a machine. She reached over to the side table to retrieve her phone, but the caller ID revealed that it wasn't her mother. It was Max. She had told half the world she wasn't getting married, but she had yet to tell him.

"Hello?" she answered, trying to keep the emotion out of her voice. She refused to cry, because she knew if she started, she wouldn't be able to stop.

"Darling," he purred in his accent. "Why am I hearing that you have canceled the cake and told the string quartet not to board their plane tomorrow?"

"Oh, that's simple, Max. I'm not going to marry you."

"Excuse me?" he sputtered, sounding genuinely surprised. "Why not? You're being foolish."

"Foolish?" She immediately felt her anger go up a tick. "I didn't think it was foolish to not marry a man who is a cheating, lying bastard."

"Cheating? I'm not cheating on you. I never have."

"You're not sleeping with Ingrid anymore? Judging by your family photo album, you looked very happy with her and your children in the South of France."

He went silent, quiet for so long that she thought he had hung up. "She told you."

"Yes. She came to see me today. Your oldest—Hugo—he looks quite like you. He's got your nose and eyes, but he has Ingrid's coloring. How the hell could you do this to me? And why the hell did you think you could get away with keeping this a secret from me?"

"I was going to tell you after we were married."

"You were going to let me walk down that aisle, thinking that I was the only woman in your life, thinking that we were going to start a family, when you knew that everything we had was a lie?"

"It wasn't a lie. Yes, I have three children. Yes, their mother is my best friend, but, darling, you are the only woman I can see myself being married to, and we are going to start a family. I've always wanted as many children as possible."

"It's hard to keep that big of a secret from the world. Others have to know. You were going to let me make a fool of myself. People have probably been laughing behind my back for years."

"Nobody would dare laugh at you. Not my chosen bride.

I'm from one of the richest and most powerful families in
the world. They respect you, and if they do not, I will make
them. So don't worry about what other people think. I will
take care of that. Now, stop this little tantrum and call everyone back. I love you. I will take care of you. You are perfect. My princess. You are meant for a grand life with me."

"You don't respect me at all—do you?" She didn't know
why she hadn't known that sooner, but the realization was
crushing. She'd spent so long with a man who she was just
an object to. "You think that this is something that I'm
just supposed to get over. You don't care about my feelings at all."

"My father has had the same mistress for over fifty
years. I have nearly a dozen half siblings. If my mother
can bear it, so can you. You're giving up so much for your
foolish American pride. This is how things work where I
come from."

"I'm not your mother," she said calmly. "And my foolish
American pride won't allow me to marry you. It's over."

"This isn't over. You'll see how sad your life is without me, and I will be waiting here for when you get over
yourself."

Ava hung up without saying any more. She had no idea
what she was going to do with the rest of her life, but she
knew that he would not be in it.

# *Chapter 3*

Derek walked up to his aunt's house as he did nearly every day after he finished his work. He had always thought of this place as his childhood home because he'd spent much more time sleeping there than at his own house. His aunt and late uncle had been like his parents. His cousin was more like his sister, and his grandmother, his most favorite person in the world, had lived there. Some of his best memories happened around the kitchen table in this house. He would say he was from a tight-knit family and mostly he was, but out of the dozens of holidays he had spent here, there were very few he could recall with his mother. She always seemed to be jetting off somewhere with a new boyfriend.

But maybe it had been better for him to be without her. His uncle was a world-famous architect who taught him how to build things and in the process be creative. He would have never thought about designing and building furniture. He would have never thought about running for mayor when he was only twenty-five years old. It still pained him a bit when he walked through the door and he realized that his uncle wouldn't be there to greet him. But this house was still a happy place. It wasn't just that it looked like a large gingerbread house; it was the fact that there was even more love in it now.

He opened the door to see his cousin's husband, Asa, sitting next to his grandmother on the couch. They were playing video games, which wasn't something he had expected to see when he walked through the door that evening.

"Are you ready to give up yet?" his grandmother, Nanny, asked Asa as she furiously pressed the buttons on her controller.

"No! How are you this good at this game? We just got it today. I think you've been practicing."

"I think you're a sore loser, or you will be in a moment when I do this finishing move on you. There, done."

Asa tossed his controller on the couch beside him and slumped in his seat. "You beat me at cards and now at this. I'm not sure I can hold my head up anymore."

Derek laughed as he walked farther into the room. Asa had just recently become a member of their family. His cousin Hallie had fallen in love with him hard after only knowing him for a month. There were a few people who thought they wouldn't make it, especially since Hallie had been engaged to another man just six months before, but Derek knew as soon as he met Asa that he was right for Hallie. He loved her unconditionally. He gave up his career as a rescue paramedic to move down to this tiny island to be with her. Derek could only respect the man for that. "What are you two up to?" he asked them.

"Playing *Street Warrior*," Nanny answered.

Nanny was active and looked much younger than her eighty years. She wasn't one of those elderly people who was going to let her age stop her.

"You all look too serious to interrupt. So I'll just find Hallie."

"She's in the kitchen with Clara." Nanny answered. "They are making dinner. Afterward, if you're prepared to battle me, I'd welcome another challenge."

Derek laughed at his feisty grandmother before he made his way into the kitchen. Hallie was stirring something, while her mother sat at the table chopping vegetables for a salad. "Hello. It smells good in here."

"Hey, Derek!" Hallie smiled at him. She was glowing. She was just a semester away from finishing her doctorate. She was enjoying being married. He had never seen her so happy. He was happy for her, but it gave him a little twinge. Not that he was jealous of her, but seeing her so in love made him realize that he never had been. He didn't necessarily want to be in love or in a serious relationship but he was thirty-three and he had never felt a strong connection to any of the women he had been involved with.

He dated. Preferred discreet relationships with divorced women, not looking for a serious commitment. He took his job as mayor very seriously. He wasn't sure how much longer he would be the mayor but as long as he was, his island would come first.

"Are my son-in-law and mother still playing that crazy fighting game?" his aunt Clara asked.

"They just finished. Nanny destroyed Asa. Apparently she an excellent street fighter."

Hallie shook her head, grinning. "Don't tell Asa, but she's had practice. You know the Johnson kid that she gives piano lessons to? Well, he got the game for his birthday, and he taught her how to play."

"She's a sly old lady, isn't she?"

"She'll outlive us all," his aunt said just before she got up from the table and left the room.

"I haven't seen you in a few days." Hallie turned down the burner and faced him. "What have you been up to?"

"We're starting to plan for founder's day down at city hall, and my own business is growing a little faster than I expected. My showroom is nearly empty."

"That's because you are an amazing craftsman. I hope you have time to make a crib for us."

His eyes widened. "Are you pregnant?"

"No. Not yet. But as soon as I'm done with school we're going to start trying. Asa isn't rushing me, but I know he's ready to be a father. I was just putting in my order now. Hopefully by the time a baby enters our lives, you'll have it done."

"Of course." He took a seat at the table. "Is anything new going on with you?"

"Not really. But I did hear that Ava Bradley canceled her wedding."

"I figured."

"You figured? It has been all over town. No one has been able to stop talking about it."

"I knew something was going on when I heard her brothers threaten to kill Vermeulen. Your husband works with her brother—he didn't tell you anything?"

She shook her head. "Just that the wedding was off. I feel bad for Ava. I had to cancel a wedding a few months before I walked down the aisle. It must be terrible to call it off when your guests have already started to arrive. Something big must have happened."

"Yes, she probably realized that he was the slimy, opportunistic scumbag that the rest of us already knew he was."

"Whoa." Hallie put her hands up in defense, but she gave him a little smile. "Tell me how you really feel about him."

The kitchen door opened and his mother, Anita, breezed in. He hadn't seen her in a few weeks, which was hard to do when they lived on an island so small.

"My baby is here!" She smiled brightly at him, but he couldn't force his lips to curl in return.

"Hi, Mom." He offered her a small, almost awkward wave. "How are you?"

She walked toward him, wearing a dress that looked more appropriate for a nightclub than a visit with her family. "I'm just great, sweetie. I'm on my way to meet my new friend. He's taking me off-island for a little wining and dining."

"That's nice," he said, not really meaning it. His mother was always with a "new friend," as she called them. She had so many boyfriends by the time he turned fifteen that he had lost count. And each time she thought they would be the one. But it had been heartbreak after heartbreak, all because she never picked the right guy. It all had started with his father. A married man who never planned to leave his wife for his young mistress, even if that young mistress did get pregnant to force his hand.

She walked over, looking at him with a mix of love and dislike as she placed her hand on his cheek. They had always had such a complicated relationship. He looked so much like his father, and he knew that he reminded her of her biggest failed relationship, reminded her of all her mistakes, reminded her that she wasn't quite good enough to make a millionaire leave his wife.

She was probably why he had never fallen in love. She had enough broken hearts for the both of them.

"How are you, Derek?" She kissed his cheek.

"I'm fine, Mom. I didn't realize you were on the island."

"I've been off and on," she said vaguely.

"I haven't seen you in a few weeks. I think we should have dinner and catch up." Things were strained between them. They always had been, and Derek knew that it would just be easier to keep her at arm's length, but he always made the effort even if it was continually rejected. She was his mother. He felt like she should be in his life.

His aunt Clara had come back into the kitchen, but his focus remained on his mother's face as he waited for her answer. Her makeup was elaborate, not distasteful, crafted to make her look more youthful. Her hair was cut precisely in some sort of asymmetrical style that was popular with the teenagers in town. She looked more like his older sister than his mother, but that's what happened when your mother was a teenager when she had you.

"Yeah, maybe next week," she said noncommittally.

It was like déjà vu, little flashbacks to when he was a kid asking her to come to his band concerts or to see him perform on the debate team, or to one of his championship soccer games when he was in college. She had always made excuses, or promises that she couldn't keep.

He nodded. Not surprised by her answer, not hurt by it, either, just curious as to what was going on in her head.

"I stopped by to see my mother. Where is she?"

"In the living room with Asa," he answered.

"See you around, kid." She winked at him and squeezed Hallie's arm before she left again.

"My baby." Aunt Clara practically pounced on him, wrapping him in a tight motherly hug. "I love you so much, Derek," she whispered. "Just like you came from me."

He closed his eyes and let himself be hugged. He knew his aunt loved him just like she loved her own child and probably twice as much as his own mother loved him. Maybe that thought should have comforted him, but it didn't. It made him feel kind of hollow.

Ava lay in bed all day. She couldn't remember the last time she had done that. Maybe she never had. She always had something to do, a task to accomplish, a job to complete, but now for the first time there was nothing ahead of her. She found that kind of terrifying.

Her stomach growled angrily at her that evening, forcing her out of bed and into the kitchen.

When she looked in the refrigerator she saw that there was nothing there but spinach and kale. Grilled chicken breasts and low-fat yogurt. It wasn't the kind of thing a woman wanted to eat after a bad breakup. A pool full of hot fudge sundae with forty gallons of whipped cream was what she needed. Or something heavy and filling, something that would momentarily take away the empty sadness.

Her mother was not coming up from Costa Rica. Ava told her to stay home, that she needed a few days of alone time to think, to regroup. But she should have let her mother come. Her mother would have cooked for her. She would have made her world-famous double chocolate cake with the thick, creamy icing. And empanadas and a huge pot of spaghetti and meatballs like she used to do when she was a child. She couldn't remember the last time she had had pasta or anything resembling a carb. She had eaten so many leafy greens that she was surprised she hadn't grown branches.

Good food was another thing that Ava had given up for Max. It was even harder than giving up her great job and the high-paying promotion she was offered just before she quit. But she wanted to look beautiful for Max on their wedding day. She had given up pie on Thanksgiving and eggnog at Christmas and grilled beef in the summer and takeout every weekend. She had lost weight for him. Nearly starved herself to fit into a dress that she didn't like.

From the kitchen she could still see it hanging on the rack. She hadn't gotten the chance to fully look at it. Ingrid's visit had stopped her in her tracks.

She didn't think it was possible to hate a garment so much, but looking at it then just served as a reminder of all the things she had given up for a man who hadn't respected her at all.

It had to go.

She walked over to it. Unlike the last time she attempted to view it, she yanked the zipper down and pulled the dress from the bag all in one motion. It was heavy, pounds and pounds of fabric and crystals and a train that would rival a princess's. Lavish, over the top, unapologetically bold. It was everything Max was, and she felt her blood start to boil. For years she had ignored the little things about him that annoyed her. She had defended him when others called him callous. She had done everything to morph herself into a wife he could be proud of, and more than she was mad at Max, she was mad at herself for being so damn stupid.

She marched out her front door and tossed the monstrous piece of fabric into the yard. It needed to be out of the house, out of her sight. Unable to taunt her, remind her of all her wasted years. But even now that it lay in the sandy dirt, she didn't feel her anger ease. So much effort had gone into that dress; so much effort had gone into building herself into a perfect woman for a man who didn't deserve her. It wasn't enough to have the dress out of the house. She stepped off the porch and kicked the dress, letting out a scream of pure frustration as she did.

It felt good to kick the dress. It felt good to let out some of the pent-up emotion she kept bottled up inside.

*Don't raise your voice.*

*Don't be too opinionated.*

*Don't ruffle feathers.*

*Be pleasant.*

*Be passive.*

She kicked the dress again. She stomped on it, like she was stomping all the years of reprogramming she had done to herself. She took pleasure in seeing the pristine white fabric getting stained a greenish brown from the grass and dirt.

But it wasn't enough.

She reached down and pulled on the bodice of the dress, feeling more satisfaction as she heard the popping of threads, but still that wasn't enough for her. The damn thing needed to be completely destroyed, all of its bad energy gone for good. She spotted a metal garbage can on the side of the house and a lonely bottle of lighter fluid meant for a charcoal grill. An idea took shape in her head.

She wondered how long it would take to barbeque a wedding dress.

Derek watched Ava from his window, completely in awe. He had gotten home from a planning meeting just a few minutes ago and was preparing to head into his workshop when he heard a strangled scream. He rushed to his window to see Ava jumping up and down on a massive pile of white fabric. He stood transfixed, unable to move, even though he knew it was wrong to watch such an intensely private moment. The Ava Bradley he had known, the incredibly put-together, icily beautiful woman, had disappeared. He was left looking at a woman so full of raw hurt and anger that even he felt the depths of it in his bones.

She was destroying her wedding dress. Her hands pulled furiously at the fabric, ripping it to shreds, little angry grunts escaping with every hard tug.

She must have had so much riding on this marriage. An entire life.

A memory of his mother flashed in his head.

Derek had been a kid, not even ten years old yet. He'd been crouched on the floor in his bedroom, staring through a crack in his door as his father told his mother that he never wanted to see her again.

*You need to get it through your head. I'm never leaving her for you.*

His father had a wife. His mother was his mistress. And that was one of the million times Derek wished he could have been born to normal parents.

But of course that wish was just too much to ask for. He watched rage take over his beautiful mother.

*I planned my life around you. I've done everything to be with you.*

And she had. Derek's father was the most important person in her world. Way more than Derek could ever hope to be.

She had hurled a vase at his father's head as he had turned to leave, letting out a guttural, primal scream as she did. Derek would never forget that sound. He would never forget how his father looked when he felt the glass shards bounce off the wall and hit his back.

*You got pregnant, forced a child on me like it was going to magically make us a family. Your plan failed. I'll take care of him, but don't ever think that he's going to turn out to be anything like my other children with you for a mother.*

His mother destroyed the house that day. Throwing lamps and chairs, ripping up photographs, stomping on keepsakes.

Derek had called his uncle Hal because he was scared and didn't know what to do, and he heard his aunt Clara's voice in the background, ordering Hal to go get him and his belongings. That was the first time he'd lived with his aunt and uncle for an extended amount of time. Over the years he had stayed with them more times than he could count.

His mind snapped back to the present when he saw Ava, dressed in a flimsy nightgown, drag the metal garbage can from the side of the house to the front yard. She hauled the dress off the ground and dumped it into the garbage can before walking away. For a moment Derek thought that

that might be it, but she came back with a can of lighter fluid and a box of matches. He watched motionlessly as she squirted the entire bottle into the can.

Something inside of Derek screamed at him to move.

He sprinted from his house and made it to Ava just as she lit a match. He caught her hand, blew it out and took the box away from her.

"Are you insane?" he shouted.

She looked up at him with shocked, angry eyes, and even though she looked crazy as hell, he still found her insanely attractive. "Are you trying to burn down the whole damn neighborhood?"

"Mind your business, Mr. Holier-Than-Thou. This doesn't concern you."

"Yes, it does! Anyone who attempts to burn down my island becomes my concern."

"Get over yourself. I'm just lighting the dress on fire. It's in a metal garbage can. It's not like I sprayed lighter fluid on your house."

"But it's windy, and you put enough fluid on there to have thirty-five cookouts. My house is full of wood and varnish and every other kind of flammable thing. There was a terrible fire on the island a few years ago that destroyed many homes. Just because you're pissed that your scumbag fiancé turned out to be an even bigger scumbag than you thought, doesn't mean you can put my house or anyone else's in jeopardy."

"The last thing I need is a lecture from you. Isn't there a dolphin you could be rescuing or a citizen you could be lecturing about their civic duty?"

"I don't lecture people. I'm just trying to stop you from being a pyromaniac lunatic!"

"All you do is lecture. It must be exhausting needing to be right every single moment of your life. Tell me, do you get nosebleeds from sticking your nose so high up in the air?"

He had never heard her speak like this; in fact, he rarely heard her speak at all, and when she did, it was in a quiet measured way. She always seemed to ooze class and elegance, and frankly she seemed like a snob to him. But today she was full of fire.

Literally and figuratively.

"Why did you choose to rent a house next to mine? There have to be dozens of rentals on this island."

"Well, excuse me, Mr. Mayor. I don't care enough to keep tabs on which house is yours, but if I had known that I would be living next door to such an insufferable jackass, I wouldn't have rented here. In fact, I would have rented a house on the other side of the island."

"Why don't you do us all a favor and go back to where you came from? This way, I won't have to worry about anything going up in flames."

"You want me to move?" Her eyes went wide as she pointed to herself. "Well, that's too damn bad, because I'm going to stay all spring and summer and possibly into fall. I'm going to throw raging keggers and hold a wet T-shirt contest and have a parade of unsavory, big-resort-building ruffians stomping through my house at all hours of the night just to piss you off. And there isn't a thing you can do about it."

"I could call the police and make a noise complaint."

She threw her head back and laughed. "You would do that, wouldn't you? I bet you were that kid in school who ratted out all the other kids. I can see the headline on the local paper now. 'Annoyed Mayor Calls Cops on Heartbroken Bride.' I'm sure your citizens will love you for it, too. Once they find out that you're living next door to the ex-fiancée of the man who tried to ruin their island, I'm sure they'll be over here with flaming pitchforks." He saw more hurt flash in her eyes. It was clearer and sharper than the anger that was radiating from her body, and it made his own anger diminish. He wasn't sure what happened between her and Vermeulen, but he knew it must have ended terribly. He almost felt bad for her.

"I wouldn't call the cops. I like to handle disputes myself."

"There won't be any more disputes—just give me back the matches. Let me have this. I need to do this."

"I'm sorry. I just can't let you risk your safety or any of the homes on this island."

"Then go to hell."

She stomped away from him then and he was left feeling...he couldn't describe it, but he knew he had never had an interaction with a woman like that before. And as he watched Ava's retreating form, he was pretty sure this wasn't going to be the last time they would be shouting at each other.

## *Chapter 4*

Ava looked at the box of chocolate-covered mint cookies in her shopping bag and realized that she hadn't bought a single ounce of organic, fresh, never-processed or frozen food. She had double-chocolate doughnuts and three kinds of chips.

She even had an entire block of cheese among her purchases because she couldn't make proper nachos without cheese. It was the first time since Maxime had proposed to her that she didn't care about watching what she ate or how many calories were in a serving size. She didn't care about getting enough protein or eating kale or how she was going to look in her wedding dress and on the arm of her handsome, rich husband. She was going to have wine tonight. Cheap seven-dollar-a-bottle wine that she really liked but had to pretend to not like to impress her ex and his snobby friends.

She was going to drink alcohol and eat ice cream with chocolate syrup and gummy worms and gnaw on a block of cheese, and she was going to enjoy every damn moment of it. As she grabbed the second junk-filled bag out of the trunk she noticed her neighbor's classic pickup truck pull into his driveway.

Ava didn't know why she hadn't known that Derek Patrick owned the house next to hers. It was odd that out of all the rentals on the island she picked the one next to his. If she had known the young mayor had lived there, she wouldn't have taken it. Things had gotten rather nasty between him and Maxime during the height of the resort debate. Max would have had a fit if he'd known she was living next door to a man he considered an enemy. But she was glad she hadn't known, because she had fallen in love with the little candy-colored cottage. The road it was on was sparsely populated and away from the busier downtown. The scenery surrounding the home was lush, with wild flowers, tall green grasses and fruit trees. She was walking distance to a small beach that was only used by the residents on this road. She could go there whenever she wanted. It was paradise. But she hadn't been to the beach the entire time she had been on the island. She hadn't taken the time to enjoy herself at all. That was going to change. She wasn't sure when she decided that she was going to stay for a long while. But it was probably around the time when Derek told her that she should move off the island.

She would stay just to spite him. Besides, she didn't have anywhere else to go.

She tried not to glance at him as he stepped out of his truck. She wasn't so sure what it was about him that rubbed her the wrong way. It wasn't the thing with Max. Any mayor going so hard to protect his island was admirable, but Derek Patrick was always just a little too good. The townspeople were full of stories about him. About how he housed a family when their home was flooded during a storm, about how he drove dialysis patients to their appointments when the community shuttle broke down. He even babysat for a single mother when her sitter canceled so that she could get to an interview. No one was that good. It just seemed unnatural. Everyone had a dark side, a bit of selfishness that ran through them from time to time, but not Derek Patrick. He was the island's golden boy, and for some reason that annoyed Ava. And it irritated her even more that he was so good-looking on top of it.

He was a big man, with broad shoulders and one of those powerful, long-stride walks that seemed to eat up the ground with each step. He certainly didn't look like any politician that she had ever seen. His clothes were constantly paint smeared, and he seemed to live in T-shirts that were just tight enough to show off his muscled upper body. He looked like a blue-collar working man.

A type of man she'd never gone out with.

He had a set of gorgeous light-bluish-greenish eyes that combined with this brown skin made him look…interesting.

Some might even say he was one of those men that was hard not to look at, and that's why Ava made it a point not to look tonight.

"Hey, Ava," she heard him say from behind. It surprised her that he would acknowledge her after their spat. "You planning on burning anything today?"

She paused and turned to look at him, annoyed with herself for doing so. He was leaning slightly against his truck, looking at her, studying her in a way that wasn't disrespectful and yet made her feel uncomfortable. It was then she realized that he had probably never seen her like this before. She lived in chic sheath dresses and designer heels. Her face was always perfectly made up, and her hair was always done. But today she wore a cheap pair of flip-flops she bought to wear on the beach and an oversize bathing suit cover-up because it was the only truly comfortable thing she had with her. He had seen her at her absolute worse the other night, and once again he was seeing her at less than her best. It bugged the hell out of her.

"The only thing I plan on burning is your house after you go to sleep tonight." She didn't know what possessed her to say that. She had never spoken to anyone like that. But she couldn't stop the flow of words. She had always been so careful to watch what she said and how she reacted when she was with Max, but she was done with that. Through with taking so much time to think about what she was going to say that she had lost out on the chance to say so many important things.

"Ouch." He frowned with a little shake of his head. "We have a big bonfire on the beach every year during the founder's day festivities. If you were a good girl, I was going to let you throw in the match to set the blaze, but since you just threatened to kill me, I'm afraid I'm going to have to give the honor to another fire-loving female."

She knew that she shouldn't respond, shouldn't engage with him any further, but she couldn't stop herself. "I wasn't going to kill you, just smoke you out. Kind of like the beady-eyed raccoon that used to live under our porch when I was a kid."

She thought she might have gone too far with that comment, but Derek surprised her and gave her an amused smile that she could only describe as sexy. His grin hit her right in the chest, and it startled her.

She was heartbroken and hurt and still reeling from the betrayal. She had no business finding any man sexy, especially the next-door neighbor, who, according to her ex, was the enemy.

She didn't return his smile; in fact, she didn't even look at him again as she walked away and into her cottage. She put the bags down on the counter, forgetting about the surely melting ice cream and picked up the phone. She dialed her sister-in-law's number.

"Can you come over here and stay with me tonight?"

"I'll be there in twenty minutes," Virginia answered without hesitation.

Ava felt relieved. She didn't want to be alone, especially when she couldn't control her feelings.

Thursdays were the day that Derek kept office hours. He was known as the mobile mayor, and instead of running the island from a stuffy old office, he'd rather get out on the island and actually see the people who lived there. Visit local businesses, talk to his residents, but he couldn't escape the office totally. So Thursdays were his days to have meetings and sign papers, approve budgets. It was his most exhausting day of the week. Sitting behind a desk drained him. It also reminded him of his father. Most of the times he saw him, the man was sitting behind a desk. Derek never wanted to be like him. Even one day a week in an office made him feel like the man he never wanted to become.

When he got home that night, he headed right to his kitchen and stared into his depressingly empty refrigerator. He couldn't remember the last time he had been grocery shopping. His usually survived the week on one of his aunt's meals. His family always sent him home with leftovers and little things they had made just for him. They spoiled him, trying to make up for all the lack of mothering in his young life. He tried to tell them that they didn't have to go through all the trouble but they seemed to like to.

He shut the door, knowing that he couldn't make a meal out of pickles and ketchup, and went in search of the dozen or so menus he kept on hand for cases like these. But before he was able to make it to the menus he heard a knock at his door. It surprised him. He lived in an extremely quiet part of town. People didn't just stop by. When he opened his front door and saw Ava Bradley standing on his porch, he became even more surprised. Ever since their little run-in over the wedding dress he'd had a hard time getting her off his mind. Of course, it wasn't every day that a man saw an elegant woman ripping her wedding dress to shreds, and it made him curious about her, made him actively think about what would make her get to that point. And then when he saw her a few days later he had literally been blown away by the way she looked. When he had gotten out of his truck, he saw her standing in her driveway wearing a little white bathing suit cover-up that barely skimmed the top of her thighs. Her hair wasn't in its normal elegantly chic style, but instead in loose, messy waves. Her face was completely clean of makeup. She was always stunningly beautiful, but that day he saw an edge to her that was probably caused by anger and pain, but it also made her damn sexy. And when he realized that what he was feeling was attraction it was like he was hit in the gut with a two-by-four. This evening was no different. She wore little cotton shorts with anchors on them and a white tank top that was so thin it was nearly see-through.

"Are you sure you're here on time?"

"Excuse me?" She blinked at him, and for the first time he noticed the color of her eyes. They were lighter than her older brother's, whose eyes seemed to be so deep brown that they were nearly black. Hers seemed almost golden.

"You said that you were going to burn down my house after I went to sleep. You're at least six hours early."

The corner of her mouth ticked up in an almost smile. He was sure she had smiled before, that she couldn't be the icily cool woman who never displayed any kind of happy emotions. Her family was too warm and loving for her to be that way, but *he* had never seen her smile. And now that he had seen just a hint of it, he wanted more, the full thing, and he wanted it all directed at him.

"I am actually here about fire," she said in her soft, nearly husky voice. "As in if you don't help me right now, I'm afraid my house will burn down."

"What?" That shook him out of his appraisal of her.

"I have an outlet that's sparking. And since you're so up on your fire safety, I figured I would come to you and skip the fire department. I didn't want to disturb you with all those pesky lights and sirens. I know how noise sensitive you are."

"You want my help?" He knew it was a dumb question, but he couldn't wrap his head around the fact that she was standing on his porch, looking disturbingly enticing.

"Yes." She nodded. "Preferably right this moment."

"Where's the outlet sparking?"

"In my kitchen."

"Do you know how to turn off the power to that room?"

"Do you think I know how to turn off the power to that room?" she retorted.

He turned away to get his toolbox. Luckily since he used the entire downstairs of his house as a work space, he didn't have to go far.

"Sorry. Stupid question. I wouldn't expect you to know how to do anything with your hands that didn't require getting your nails done."

"I can do a lot of good things with my hands. Unfortunately, you'll never learn what those things are."

Her words nearly stopped him in his tracks, and a vivid but all-too-brief image of her running her hands down his bare chest flashed in his mind. He shouldn't be thinking about her that way. He didn't want to be thinking about her that way. She represented a type of woman he couldn't stand. "If it includes using Google to find your next rich boyfriend, I'm not interested."

"Forget it." She sighed and stepped off the porch. "I'll call the fire department. Let's just hope a strong gust of wind doesn't carry one of those errant sparks to your house."

"I didn't say I wasn't going to help you." He caught her wrist with his free hand just as she turned to walk away, ignoring how incredibly soft her skin was and the tiny little charge he felt when his skin connected with hers. "Besides, if you called the fire department over this, I would never hear the end of it from the guys."

"It's not your job to fix electrical problems."

"No." He walked ahead of her to her house, trying to shake off the weird feeling that was rolling around within him. He had been in the house many times before the original owner decided to rent it out and move to the retirement community on the island. He knew where the fuse box was, and as he approached the steps he once again found himself surprised that Ava Bradley had picked this house when she could have rented any of the luxurious oceanfront rentals the island had to offer. The last time he had been here it was decorated in a style that he could only describe as old lady chic. There had been a lot of pink and floral print; he could see it had been redecorated.

The first word that came to Derek's mind was *cozy*. There were big, overstuffed couches and chairs, little odds and ends that gave the place a touch of elegance. He would have thought she preferred sleek lines and modern furniture that was more artistic than functional. But she was staying in a place that looked more like a home than a rental. He even glimpsed a family photograph on the bookshelf as he walked through.

He looked over his shoulder to see that she was directly behind him. A little mischievous voice in his head told him to stop short, just so she would crash into him, but he didn't do it.

"You don't have to follow so close. I'm not going to steal anything. I'm here to help you, remember?"

"I'm not about to let a strange man loose in my house. Especially one who already seems to know his way around it."

"Stranger? I've known your brother for years. I'm the mayor and probably the most well-known person in this town."

"I didn't say stranger. I said strange. And, sweetheart, you are the definition of the word."

He grinned at her. He couldn't stop himself. Maybe he was a sadist, but her biting remarks did something to him. No one ever spoke to him that way. Every citizen of Hideaway Island was unfailingly polite to him. But she wasn't. It was...refreshing. "Come here. Let me show you how to shut off the power in case this ever happens again. This house is old—the wiring might need to be completely replaced."

"Don't say that," she groaned. "I don't want to move out."

"Let me check first, but even if it comes to that, it won't take that long, and your brother lives on the island. His house is so large—they probably wouldn't see you for days."

"He would make sure he saw me. Since I called off my wedding he's been so worried about me that he calls me twice a day to make sure I haven't flung myself off a bridge."

"From what I saw the day it went down, I'm surprised he didn't toss that jackass off the bridge."

"I'm sure he would have, but my sister-in-law has a calming effect on him."

She couldn't hide the sadness in her eyes, and something tugged in his chest. He didn't want to feel bad for her, so he turned to the box, opened the door and shut off the power to the kitchen. "Come here." He pointed to the clearly labeled switches without looking at her to see if she understood. He didn't want to see any more of her hurt.

"Do you have candles?"

"Yes."

"Would you mind lighting some in the kitchen?"

"I hope this isn't your way of setting the mood, because whatever you're thinking, it's not going to happen."

"Do you think every man on the planet wants you, because I can assure you that they don't," he said, lying through his teeth. A man would be crazy not to want her. "Which outlet is it?"

"The one closest to the stove."

He nodded. "Get the candles and meet me in there. I'm going to need the extra light to see."

"Maybe I should leave the power off and call the property manager in the morning."

"I'm here. Might as well take a look."

She walked away to get the candles, and he took a deep breath. It was much harder to breathe when she was in the same space as him.

# Chapter 5

Ava watched Derek as he removed the cover plate and shined his light into the outlet. His bicep bunched beneath his T-shirt, and he moved with such assuredness that she found it hard not to stare. She should have removed herself to another room completely, but she couldn't force herself to go. It was a novelty seeing a man who could work with his hands. Maxime's hands were softer than hers. Elias was a surgeon and very good with his hands, but she had never seen her twin fix anything. Carlos, either. The last man she had seen actually work with his hands was her father. He changed his own oil and repaired the roof, built their deck. He could do anything. Ava didn't think they made men like him anymore, but there was Derek, removing the outlet with the skill of an electrician.

"How do you know how to do this stuff? Did your father teach you or something?" He turned and looked at her, hardness in his eyes.

He didn't like her; there was no mistaking it. She didn't

like him, either, and she had wanted to stand there quietly as he worked, but she was getting tired of being alone with her thoughts. She didn't want to be around her family or friends because she knew they would feel sorry for her and she didn't want or need that. She wasn't the delicate flower the world made her out to be.

"No," he spoke as he turned back to his work. "I'm not sure my father would know a screwdriver from a wrench. In fact, I'm pretty sure his leather office chair is permanently fused to his behind."

"Oh." She had touched on a nerve. But that still didn't explain how he learned. "You taught yourself?"

"Partly. It was just my mother and I, and when I got to be a teenager, it was only me. You learn how to do things when you have no other choice."

"Oh," she said again, feeling a little dumb. "I'm sorry."

He glanced back at her, something flashing in those bluish eyes that she couldn't read. "Don't be. I can't take all the credit. My uncle taught me how to be a man. As far as I'm concerned, he's my real father."

"You must be very close."

"We were. He died almost two years ago."

"It doesn't get any easier, does it?" she asked. "My father died just after we graduated from college. I still pick up the phone to call him, only to realize that he won't be able to answer." She had done that recently. She had wanted to know the name of the little seafood place he used to take them to, and as she dialed it struck her. And it devastated her all over again.

"No. It doesn't. It never gets easier," he answered softly.

The doorbell rang, causing Ava to jump. She was glad for the distraction. Things had gotten too real and too deep with a man she barely knew.

"Are you expecting someone?"

"Yes." She rushed from the room and answered the door

to find a pizza delivery guy standing there. He was a teen-ager in a tank top, board shorts and long blondish hair covered by a baseball cap with the pizzeria's logo on it.

"You having a party or something?" he asked her as he handed her the three boxes.

"Nope. Just a bad few weeks."

"I find that cheesy bread makes the world a brighter place." He grinned at her, and she tipped him generously before returning to the kitchen, which was lit only with the scented white candles and the glow of Derek's flashlight.

She had had dozens of candlelight dinners with Max, but somehow this seemed more intimate. She had never talked to Max about her father, about how much it had hurt to lose him. They had been together for three years, and it had never come up.

"You shouldn't have any more problems. This outlet was installed incorrectly. I don't think you'll need the wiring replaced, but to be on the safe side I'll call my friend to come take a look."

"You don't have to do that. I can make the call. One of the things I can do with my hands really well is dial a phone."

He gave her a little smile and shook his head. "Let me. I know who does the best work in town. He'll be here first thing in the morning."

"Thank you. I appreciate that."

"Is that gratitude from you? I must admit that I'm shocked. I was half expecting you lured me here to club me over the head."

"Why would I do that? Planning something like that would require wasting my precious thoughts on you."

"Things got pretty intense between me and your fiancé. I was fairly sure he had put a hit out on me. I've never seen a face go that purple with rage when I told him he was never going to be able to build on this island."

"And you thought that me canceling my wedding, attempting to destroy my dress and telling you my outlet sparked was an elaborate ruse to get you into my clutches so I could carry out some nefarious plan?"

"Well, when you say it like that, it sounds stupid."

Laughter escaped her. It startled her because she wasn't expecting it. She couldn't remember the last time she had really laughed. Even before things came crashing down around her.

"You don't bring that out often, do you?" He looked at her; there was no smile on his face, no softness to his expression.

"What?"

"That smile. It could knock a lesser man on his ass."

She didn't know how to react to his comment. If he was hitting on her, it would have been all too easy for her to throw him out, but he wasn't hitting on her. She wasn't sure what he said was a compliment at all.

"Do you like pizza?"

"That is probably the dumbest question you've ever asked."

"Everyone likes pizza, don't they?" She reached into the cabinet for some plates.

"If they don't I would have them investigated because they clearly are up to no good."

"I couldn't decide between the veggie lover and the meat lover, so I asked them to put both on one jumbo pie. I also got cheesy bread and cinnamon sticks with cream cheese icing," she said as she placed food on his plate.

"No chicken wings?"

She gasped. "I haven't had chicken wings in years. Should I call back?"

"I was joking." He took the plate from her, his fingers brushing her hand as he did. She wasn't sure what she had felt when he grabbed her wrist earlier, but now as they touched again she definitely knew that there was a little charge there.

She couldn't explain why she was feeling it when she was still so wrecked from the breakup. She wasn't looking for a rebound or a man to make her forget. Yes, Derek was tall, strong and very good-looking, but she lived in Miami among some of the world's most beautiful men and she had felt absolutely nothing around them.

He put his plate down and went to the cabinet to get glasses. "Let me get you something to drink."

"I've got wine, water and chocolate milk. I don't really want water right now."

"Wine it is."

"There's some in the refrigerator."

"I love this kind," he said as he took a bottle from the refrigerator. "My grandmother says I should be ashamed of myself for liking such cheap stuff, but if I have to drink wine over beer, this is the brand I'm picking."

She grabbed the plates and brought them to the kitchen table as he was pouring them large glasses. "I guess it's safe to admit that I like ice in my wine, too."

Derek grinned widely at her. "So does my aunt Clara. We don't tell my grandmother, though. If you want ice in your wine, you'll have ice in your wine."

Ava smiled back at him. She was annoyed with herself for finding it hard to dislike him. Everyone liked him. The entire island was devoted to him, and she was starting to see why. He was easy to be around.

She took her first bite of pizza as he took the chair beside her. For a moment all she could do was sit there and moan. Hot, gooey cheese, spicy sausage and fresh veggies all in one bite. She could remember the last time she had pizza. It was almost two years ago now, and she had been with her brothers. It was right before Carlos had met Virginia. Then it was frozen pizza that Carlos had in his house, but she still loved every bite of it. It was so rare that she allowed herself to enjoy what she was eating.

"I'm surprised to see you eat like that, Ava." Derek was watching her, she could feel his eyes on her as she ate, but she didn't care. She was too focused on her food. "I would have thought you would be eating something green."

"I'm sick of green stuff. I don't ever want to take another sip of unsweetened green tea, or have a kale smoothie, or eat another salad with no dressing. I was nearly starving myself so that I would look good in my wedding dress, so that I would look good for him. I'm done with that now, and all I want to eat is pizza and cookies and things with more calories than I should consume in a week." She took another huge bite of pizza and washed it down with a large gulp of wine.

"You are beautiful, Ava. There is no denying that, but I thought you seemed a little too skinny."

"Did I ask you what you thought?"

"Nope, but I'm telling you that starving yourself for a man is stupid, and if he didn't appreciate you the way you were, you should have sent his ass packing a long time ago."

He was right about that. Max never told her that she had to look a certain way. It was simply expected. *Be thin. Be fit. Be fashionable.*

Her mother was incredibly curvy. The women in her family weren't thin. Her weight had been a huge struggle for years.

They ate in quiet for a while. It should have been an awkward silence, but for her it wasn't.

"So are you going to tell me why you ended it? I can list a dozen reasons you should have, but I would like to hear it from you."

Ava picked up her glass and took a long sip. "Max has a secret family."

"What?" Derek sat up straight. "There were a million

things I thought you were going to say. None of them were that."

"He has three children. The oldest one is practically an adult."

"How did you find out?"

"Ingrid, his mistress, came here a couple of weeks ago to tell me. She had a photo album full of candid pictures of Max and his kids."

"Mistress…he's still sleeping with his children's mother?"

"Yes. He loves her. There was a picture of them together. They were laughing. His arm was wrapped around her. The look of love on his face was undeniable. He's never looked at me that way. Not even once." She felt herself growing emotional, and her eyes filled with tears. She tried to hold them back. She hadn't cried yet. She had refused to. Max wasn't worth it, but she was feeling too much at the moment.

"Ava." Derek reached across the table and took her hand. The simple gesture was more comforting than it should have been.

"He was never going to tell me about them. If she hadn't come here, I would have walked down the aisle like an idiot thinking that every time he went away, he was going on a business trip."

"If he loves her, then why did he ask you to marry him?"

"He was using me. I fit the image. Ingrid doesn't."

"So she came here to get back at you?"

"No. She thought I should know that we would be sharing him. I guess she thought having everything out in the open would be for the best. She was quite distressed when I told her that I wasn't going to marry him."

"She still expected you to marry him?"

"Of course, and so did he." She swiped at the tears rolling down her cheeks. "He always gets what he wants. I'm not a person to him. I'm property. I was supposed to be happy spending his money and doing as he wished. I'm not supposed to be angry. I'm supposed to feel lucky that he chose me to spend the rest of his life with."

"Ava…" His arms came around her, and he pulled her from her chair and into his lap. She felt protected then. Completely safe. She couldn't remember the last time she'd felt this way.

Actually, she could. It was before he father had died.

"I thought I was going to spend the rest of my life with him, and he doesn't even love me. I'm such an idiot."

"No, you aren't. I saw the way he treated you, like you were a precious stone. He loves you in his own way. But a man like that is incapable of true, deep love. Because there is something broken inside of him. You didn't do anything wrong. You expected him to love you the way you loved him. That's what every woman should expect of the man she is going to spend the rest of her life with."

His sweet words made her cry even harder, and she hated him for that. It had been a full two weeks since she had called off her wedding, and she had been holding it together for all that time. But Derek had come and made her think about her father and made her feel safe when she no longer thought that was a feeling she could have, and it undid her.

He held her, rubbing his big hand down her back. She wasn't sure how long she cried, but she felt his lips graze her cheek. It felt nice. Warm. Comforting.

"You'll find a new man," he whispered. "One that will love you." He kissed her cheek. It was a soft peck, which was probably given to be kind, but as she lifted her head to say something to him, his mouth moved closer and his lips brushed against hers.

Before she had felt an electrical charge when they had touched, a little humming that told her there might be something there. The moment his lips pressed against hers she felt a full zap to her system, and instead of moving away from him, she moved closer to him and allowed him to kiss her again. She allowed him to deepen that kiss. She allowed herself to kiss him back. It was only a moment before she came to her senses and realized what was happening.

"What the hell are you doing?" She jumped off his lap. "Why did you kiss me? Who told you that you could kiss me?" She swiped her hand across her lips, hoping to remove the warm, tingling feeling that he had put there with his mouth. She had never been kissed like that before, never felt that way after she had been kissed. It was like he performed some sort of witchcraft on her.

"You're wiping your mouth?" He raised a brow. "It was that bad?"

"Yes. You're a terrible kisser. It was gross. I need to gargle with bleach. Get out."

"Get out?"

"Yeah, get out, Mr. Grabby-Hands-Kissy-Mouth."

"You were… I was…" He let out a sound of pure frustration, grabbed his toolbox and stormed out of the room. A moment later she heard the front door slam. She collapsed into her chair then, relieved.

She had no business kissing him.

And certainly no business wanting it to happen over and over again.

The next day Derek took the ferry to Miami. He needed to get some supplies for his furniture business, but the real reason he had gone off-island was to visit Mariel. Mariel was divorced and in her early forties with a kid in college. They had been casually seeing each other for years since they'd met at a dinner for Florida entrepreneurs. She didn't want anything from him. Not a relationship, not a commitment, not even much of his time. It was the perfect arrangement. She was smart, funny, good in bed and focused on growing her business. She understood that his work came first. She was exactly the kind of woman he needed in his life.

"I'm a little surprised to see you, Derek. It's been a while." They sat on her patio. She was sitting across from him in a designer chair, her legs crossed seductively, a high-heeled red shoe dangling from her foot. It should have turned him on immensely, but he was distracted.

"Is this not a good time?"

"It is always a good time when you are here. I haven't seen you in a few months. I thought you might've moved on to younger pastures."

"No. I've been busy. This is the first chance I've gotten to get off-island in weeks."

"Oh? I'm not sure how you do it. I'd go crazy if I had to wait for a ferry to escape someplace."

"It's not escaping. I love it there. There isn't a place on earth that can compare to Hideaway Island."

"Yes. It's beautiful, but if you want good shopping or exciting nightlife, it's not exactly the place to be. You're a young man, Derek. A beautiful, talented young man. If you came to Miami after your term is over, I think you would love it here. You would be stepping over women."

"I'm not looking to step over women. I just need one good one in my life." Ava's face annoyingly flashed in his mind for the hundredth time that day. He could not stop thinking about her. It was the real reason he had gone off-island today. To escape his thoughts of her. But she had still managed to follow him.

Last night had been so weird. He had planned to go over there to check her outlet and then leave, but somehow they ended up having dinner together. Just pizza and cheap wine, but in that candlelit kitchen it was the most intimate dinner he'd had in years.

He had gone hard watching her take that first bite of her

pizza. She closed her eyes, let out a little moan, reacted as if what she had in her mouth tasted heavenly. He would never forget that sound or the expression on her face. It made him wonder what she would look like in bed as a man worked between her legs. Would she make that same face, close her eyes the same way, give that little moan that would be the end to a weaker man?

He was getting hard thinking about her again. "Come here," he said to Mariel, hoping that a couple of hours with her would banish thoughts of his neighbor from his mind.

She stood up, long, toned legs looking fantastic in the short dress she wore. She walked over to him with the strides of a practiced seductress. Most men would have been jelly by now, but watching her come closer to him wasn't making his heart race. He wasn't overcome with the urge to take her to her bedroom and strip her naked.

He wasn't really feeling anything for her.

"I always like your visits," she said as she slid onto his lap. Immediately he noticed the difference between the way she felt and the way Ava had felt last night. Mariel was long and lanky like a model. Ava was more petite, and heavier, but in a good way. Her round bottom had felt so delicious in his lap, like it was meant to be there.

"I like my visits here, too. I should make an effort to come see you more."

"You should. Or maybe I can come to the island sometimes."

"No," he said quickly without meaning to.

"No? Are you embarrassed to be seen with me?"

"You are gorgeous and successful. I wouldn't be embarrassed at all. But I'm the mayor of a small island, and if my grandmother and aunts saw me with you, they would be planning our wedding and asking you when you planned on getting pregnant."

"Oh." She shook her head. "That won't do."

"My town has been interested in marrying me off for some time now."

"What good is a mayor without a perfect first lady?"

"Exactly. It's hard to be discreet there."

"Well, this is one place you don't have to be discreet," she said before she pressed her lips to his.

*Goddamn it.*

He had kissed Ava for only a moment and yet her kiss came rushing back to the forefront of his mind. She freaked out and threw him out of her house, but before she did, she had kissed him back. Warm, soft, full lips. A little breathy sigh. Her arms wrapped around him. It was a beautiful kiss, even if she had said it was disgusting.

She was right. He shouldn't have kissed her. Especially since she was two weeks single, fresh from a long relationship. But he couldn't help himself. He couldn't imagine what she was feeling and yet when he looked into her big brown eyes he could see how hurt she was; he could feel it. She thought that she was unlovable. That she was some kind of prop. Derek couldn't stand seeing her that way, and something in his brain shouted, *Make it better.*

*Make her better.*

She'd come easily when he pulled her onto his lap. She'd held on to him as she cried, and this incredible need to protect her had come over him.

He should have had the opposite reaction. He had been with his mother through many of her breakups. He had heard her cry and rage and fall apart so many times, he had almost become numb to it.

There were similarities between the two women. Both beautiful. Both chose rich men who they should have known weren't right for them. Both changed who they were to fit a man's expectations. Derek's heart should have hardened to her. He should have thought that she got what she deserved for getting involved with a man who was so clearly a snake. But there was one major difference between his mother and Ava. He felt in his gut that Ava wouldn't repeat her mistake.

"Um, Derek?" Mariel had pulled her lips from his and frowned down at him. "Is there something wrong? You seem like you're not enjoying this."

"No." He moved his lips closer to her again. "I am." He could push through this and make love to her. It had been a couple of months since he last had sex. He probably needed to blow off steam. But as she wrapped her arms around him, he knew it wouldn't be fair to Mariel if he did, because he would go to bed with her while his mind was on another woman. "I'm sorry." He sighed. "I can't do this today."

Mariel nodded and gave him a small smile. "I knew this day would come. It always does with the younger ones."

"What?"

"You've outgrown this. You need a partner, not a sex buddy. Maybe your family is right. It is time for you to find a first lady."

Ava sat on her porch swing that evening, her mind peacefully blank for once. There was a warm breeze blowing and the sound of birds chirping in the distance. She felt languid. She wasn't sure how that was possible, but she did. She had spoken to her mother for more than an hour on the phone that day and made plans with Elias for that weekend. Her underlying sadness was still there, but overall she had felt pretty good. If she had gone back to Miami, she was sure this wouldn't be possible. There must be something special about Hideaway Island.

She saw Derek's truck pull up, and for a moment she debated going inside so she didn't have to speak to him. But she didn't feel like moving, and she didn't want to avoid him today. So she sat there and when he got out of his truck she made eye contact with him and waved. He started walking over to her, and as he got closer she immediately noticed how tired he looked. He didn't say a word to her as he dropped himself beside her on the porch swing.

She tried to ignore the tingles that rushed along her skin when she felt his warm, heavy body brush against hers. He had kissed her last night—more than that, he had held her while she had cried. No one had seen that side of her, emotional and stripped down. She had admitted things about her relationship with Max that she hadn't told anyone else.

He said nothing for a long time, just sat next to her as they swayed on the swing. She wondered what was going through his head. Had he thought about their kiss? She had freaked out. He had no right to kiss her when she had been so vulnerable. But after replaying it in her head a hundred times, she couldn't muster up enough energy to be mad at him. He hadn't been trying to take advantage of her. He had been comforting her, and it did make her feel better. Maybe she had just needed to cry.

"Thank you for calling your electrician friend. He came over first thing this morning."

"Was everything okay?"

"Yes, but I was surprised to see him after last night. I didn't think you would call."

"Why? Because you said I was gross and kicked me out of your house after I fixed your potential fire hazard?"

"I didn't call you gross."

"You said you needed to gargle with bleach."

"And I did. I don't know where you have been."

"I don't like you," he said. "I like everyone, but I really, really don't like you."

"I don't like you, either. Calling your friend to come check my wiring made me dislike you even more."

"Keeping my promises offends you?"

"Yes. I wouldn't have called for you. You always take the higher ground, and I find that incredibly annoying. It's no wonder you're single. No woman could ever be good enough for you."

"That's not true."

"Yes. It is. Why don't you become a priest? Then it'd be your job to make people feel guilty."

"I like sex too much to become a priest. I'm pretty sure having so many impure thoughts would disqualify me."

"You think about sex a lot, do you?"

"Don't you?" He looked over at her.

"Yes," she admitted, but she didn't know why. "Why don't I ever hear about you with a woman? This town talks. But your image is squeaky-clean. Are you sure you don't have any kinky skeletons in your closet?"

"I was involved with someone off-island, but it wasn't serious. It's over now."

"What about on-island? I'm sure there are single women here who would love to be involved with you."

"I never sleep with constituents. It'd be one thing if I was looking for a serious relationship, but I'm not. I love this island too much to have my personal needs affect how I run it."

"No island booty calls for the mayor." She nodded. "Got it."

"I used to have a thing for your sister-in-law."

"You did?" she asked, but she wasn't surprised. Virginia was beautiful and brilliant.

"Yeah. She loves my furniture, and she's gorgeous. I would have married her."

"Why didn't things work out?"

"I think you know the answer to the question. Your brother was already in love with her. He didn't know it, but I could tell by the way he looked at her."

"He does love her. He loves her like my father loved my mother. I think seeing Carlos and Virginia together made me realize that my relationship with Max wasn't how it should be. But I ignored it. I made excuses for him and fooled myself into thinking that Max was the way he was because he was European. Why do I keep talking to you about this?" She ran her hand over her face.

"It's not your fault." He bumped her shoulder with his. "I've been told I have a kind face."

"A kind of face that makes me want to vomit."

His expression turned horrified. "You're mean."

She grinned at him. "I know. You bring it out in me."

A delivery truck pulled up. Ava thought that maybe Derek was expecting a package, but the driver walked up to her house and handed her a small box. She wasn't expecting anything. She held the box in her hand for a few moments. She had a sneaking suspicion who it was from, even though the return address didn't say. She should have sent it back with the driver, but he was long gone.

She handed it to Derek. "Will you open this for me?"

He took the box from her hands, his fingers brushing hers again as he did. She held her breath as he tore open the box to reveal a ring box. Max was sending back her engagement ring. But it wasn't her engagement ring. It was a different ring altogether.

"A pink diamond," Derek said, taking it out of the box and lifting it up to study it. "I've never actually seen one before, and I never thought they could ever come in this size."

Ava shut her eyes. "He thinks he can buy me back."

"He does." She heard paper rustling but refused to look. "There's a note. 'Maybe you'll like this one a little better—M.'"

"He doesn't know me at all, does he? He thinks I was only marrying him for his money."

"Screw him. You're better off without him." She felt Derek's hand slide into hers. "You hungry? I feel like seafood. Come on."

She looked at him. "I look terrible." She had put on

weight in the past two weeks since she had begun her junk-food binge. Her tight, structured sheath dresses were no longer fitting her properly, so she had gone to a store in town and picked up a bunch of sundresses that she found on the clearance rack. Her hair was a mess in its natural state. Her face hadn't seen a lick of makeup in weeks. She didn't feel like the woman she had been for so long. But for so long so much of her identity had been tied into the way that she looked.

"You're beautiful, Ava," he said sincerely, and it did something funny to her stomach. He stood up and tugged on her hand, and the next thing she knew she was inside Derek's pickup truck.

They pulled up to the little seafood shack on the water her father had taken them to when she was a kid, the same place she had attempted to call her father about.

She looked over at Derek, feeling a rush of emotion. He had gotten into her head somehow. And she didn't know if she hated it or if it was exactly what she needed.

## Chapter 6

He hadn't planned this. To be here with Ava tonight, but when he saw her on the porch and they locked eyes he couldn't force his feet to go in the direction of his house.

Hack's Shack wasn't anything fancy. It was just a shed directly on the water that served the best seafood on the island. He didn't ask her what she wanted. She was distracted, still hurting from her jerk ex-fiancé's move of sending her a bigger ring. So he ordered them two beers, two seafood chowders and a Hack's Feast, which was composed of shrimp, white fish, clams and scallops served over a large bed of seasoned French fries.

They didn't speak much, ate mostly in silence as they listened to the waves gently hit the shore. It was nearly empty there, and Derek was glad, because there wouldn't be too many people to witness him taking in Ava. She said she looked a mess, but he thought she was beautiful. She wore a blush-pink sundress that made her look sweet and innocent. Her wavy hair was grazing her chin and blew slightly in the breeze. She was sexy. It was the way she held her head, and walked and spoke and looked at him beneath her long lashes. She was clearly heartbroken and he shouldn't want her so badly, but he did. It was just one of those things he was going to have to accept.

"Did you know I loved it here?" she asked him as she bit into a fry.

"Yes. I broke into your house and read your diary."

She smiled softly at him. *Beautiful.* He would pay to see that smile more often. "I guess you wouldn't. My father used to take us here when we were kids. I wasn't sure it was still around."

"It'll be around forever. I made it a law. As mayor I can do stuff like that."

"You're such a dork."

"I know. I want this island to stay exactly like it is. I know every place has to evolve over time, but it needs to evolve in the right way."

"Which is why you fought so hard to prevent Max from building that resort here."

He nodded. "I had to go against half of the city council. It would have brought more revenue to the island, but we don't need the money. A resort that huge would have changed things. This place wouldn't have felt like home anymore."

"You don't have to convince me. You and your islanders practically ran Max out of town. I hope you realize that you were the source of our only big fight."

"Was I? Did you tell him that you thought I was sexy and that you dreamed of being with me at night instead of him?"

"Don't flatter yourself, buster. Max didn't want to get married here after he didn't get what he wanted. I did. It was important to me, and I told him if I didn't get what I wanted, I wouldn't marry him."

"Total diva move. It doesn't surprise me."

"You really think I'm a stuck-up little brat, don't you?"

"Yes." He nodded. "Or at least I did."

"Is your opinion of me changing?"

"Yes, but I still don't like you. You are very mean to me."

She gifted him with another smile. "Somebody needs to be mean to you. It will keep you humble."

"Derek?" He heard his name being called by a familiar voice, and he turned to see his mother walking toward him. She was with a much younger man. Derek would put the guy in his late twenties. It was a departure for his mother, who usually liked her men older and much richer.

"Hey." He stood as she approached, and they awkwardly hugged each other. She wore only a sheer cover-up, and through it he could see her leopard-print bikini. She wore spiked gold heels, and he wished that she'd dress like his aunts, who were all beautiful and tasteful.

"How are you, sweetheart?"

"Fine. And yourself?"

"Been keeping busy. I want you to meet my friend Perry. He's from a family of jewelers. Look at the earrings he got for me." She motioned to her diamond studs.

"Nice. It's good to meet you, Perry."

"Likewise." The guy nodded.

A long moment of painful silence followed. "Well, we're just here to pick up our order, and then we're heading back to Perry's rental."

"Sounds fun. Have a good time."

"I'll speak to you later, sweetheart?"

"Yes. All you have to do is call." He would always keep the door open, but he wasn't going to keep bending over backward only to get the same result. She could meet him halfway. "Goodbye."

"Goodbye, sweetheart."

He sat down again, facing Ava, who was looking at him with naked curiosity. "You didn't introduce me. Are you afraid your citizens are going to stone you for hanging out with the stuck-up ex of Maxime Vermeulen?"

"I don't care who knows I'm with you." The truth was he didn't introduce her because he hadn't thought to. When his mother was around, his mind went blank. "You want dessert? They make amazing cake here. Tonight they have cream cheese swirled German chocolate and orange cream cake, which tastes like a creamsicle."

"I obviously want both. Duh. Who was that woman? You seemed incredibly tense around her. Or maybe you are just tense around all women who wear leopard-print bikinis to dinner. It is a bold statement."

"That was my mother," he admitted.

"Oh. I'm sorry."

"That she's my mother? Don't be sorry. That thought might have crossed my mind a time or two." He couldn't believe that he had said those words aloud. Ava seemed to have some kind of weird power over him. It was the first time in his life he could say whatever popped in his mind without fear.

"I'm sorry I was disrespectful about her."

"You weren't. If you're going to apologize for something, you should tell me you're sorry for eating all the scallops."

Her eyes twinkled a little as she smiled. "I'm not sorry for that. I would do it again. Go get us cake, Derek. Let's get it to go."

"As you wish, madam."

Moments later they were back in his truck and heading home.

"Wait," Ava said as they pulled onto their road. "Can we stop at the beach before we go back?"

"Yeah." He was glad that she suggested it because as weird as this day was, he didn't want it to be over just yet.

"I haven't been here yet," she said, looking at the ocean.

"No? This little beach is exactly why I bought the house."

"There are few things in life that are perfect, and this is one of them."

"Something we agree on."

She reached for the bag with the cake in it and handed him one of the boxes and a fork. For a while they just sat in silence, watching the sun set over the ocean as they ate. He had never been with a woman like this before, where words weren't needed. It was nice.

"Thank you for today," she said so softly he could barely hear her. "You're a good man, Derek Patrick."

"Was that a compliment from you? I must be dying."

"Shut up, jerk."

"That's more like it." He winked at her.

"I'm so full I could burst."

"Hack's doesn't skimp on the portions. Are you ready to go home? You can eat the rest of your cake for breakfast."

She nodded. "Cake for breakfast is the best part of being an adult."

He started his truck and made the short drive back home. They stepped out and he was prepared to walk her to her door, but she stopped him when she placed a hand on his chest.

"This means nothing," she said to him just before she pressed her lips to his. It was one sweet, simple kiss that he wanted to repeat again and again.

"I thought you didn't like kissing me."

"I don't. I find it incredibly repulsive, and I need to gargle with bleach again. But I just wanted to say thank you for tonight."

"You're welcome, Ava."

She walked away from him then, and he knew without a doubt that he was going to make love to her before she left the island.

* * *

"Hey, snot face." Elias walked up to her a couple of days later. She could tell he had just come from the hospital because he was still in his scrubs. All Elias ever did was work. He was a young surgeon and on his way to becoming a brilliant one, but sometimes Ava worried about him.

He had no social life to speak of. She wanted love for her brother. He was full of macho swagger and claimed that he was perfectly happy on his own, but she wanted someone to take care of him, someone to love him. She'd thought about him a lot when she was about to marry Max. She knew she wouldn't see him as much because she was supposed to be splitting her time between the States and Europe. But they had never lived more than a house away from each other. And as Elias got further into his career, she saw him become more and more serious. She was worried about no one reminding him that he needed to take time to have fun. But she guessed she didn't have to worry about them being apart anymore. One of the best parts of finding out her fiancé was a lying cheater was that she didn't have to be away from her family.

"Hey, big head."

He sat next to her on her porch swing and leaned against her slightly. His exhaustion was clear, and she felt bad that he'd made the trip from Miami to be with her today. "You could have canceled. I would have understood."

"I told you I was coming, and now I'm here."

"How was work?" she asked him, watching him close his eyes.

"I was in surgery all night. Multilevel spinal fusion. I've never seen one, so I asked the chief of surgery if I could scrub in and assist. There was scar tissue and unexpected complications. I learned a lot, but, damn, was that a long surgery."

"I've got a spare bedroom. Go to sleep. You're no fun when you're tired."

"I bought my overnight bag. I'm staying the weekend." He opened his eyes and looked at her. "How are you feeling?"

"Okay, I guess. Max sent a bigger ring. I sent it back. This morning I got a bracelet and a necklace and three dozen roses. I tossed them in the garbage."

"He hasn't tried to call you?"

"I'm sure he has. I've blocked his number."

"He hasn't come to see you?"

"No, not yet."

"You should let me kill him. I'm a surgeon. I can dismember a body like nobody's business."

"That's horrifying and slightly comforting. Let the weasel live. His children need him."

"I got you a present." He got up and walked to his car. "It's no diamond ring, but I saw it and thought of you."

"A present?" She clapped her hands.

He pulled a Hula-Hoop and a jump rope out of the car. She got up from her seat and met him in the yard. She was feeling ridiculously close to tears again. It was the most thoughtful present he had ever given her.

"I'm finally replacing it. The jump rope is interest."

The first summer they had come to the island on vacation, Elias had broken her Hula-Hoop. She told him if he didn't replace it, she would never speak to him again. Twenty-two years later he had finally come through.

"Eli." She looked at her twin for a long moment, afraid she couldn't find the right words to thank him. "I don't think I can handle you being nice to me. I'm not used to it."

"I'm not being nice to you. I broke it. You do realize that I'm now expecting you to replace my GI Joes that you stole."

"Okay. I'll just return the gorgeous watch I was going to give you for our birthday."

"No. I still want that. Sometimes a man needs a just-because present."

"I'm not even sure they make GI Joes anymore."

"eBay, baby."

She shook her head and grinned at him. "Let me try this out. I haven't done this since I was a kid." After a shaky start, she got the hang of it. She couldn't remember the last time she had done something for the simple joy of it.

She giggled. She hadn't done that since she was a girl.

"You're pretty good at that, Ava."

The sound of Derek's voice made her look up. He was standing just to the side of her, a little smirk on his face and a look in his eyes that…that…well, it made her stop Hula-Hooping.

"You sneaky creeper. I didn't even see you walk over."

"You were having too much fun." He turned his attention to Elias. "How are you, Elias? It's good to see you. If you are ever looking to make your home on this island, our hospital would be lucky have you."

"That's a nice offer, and I might be looking to retire here, but my specialty is going to be trauma surgery. This island is the not exactly a hotbed for trauma."

"Understood. But the offer is always open."

"Thank you. I've been up for twenty-four hours. Please excuse me. I'm going to crash for a while."

"Will you be up in time to have dinner with me?" Ava asked him.

"I can't promise you that. I'm probably going to sleep the sleep of the dead. Derek, have dinner with my sister. I think she's lonely."

"I'm not lonely!"

"I'll have dinner with her." Derek assured him without

even looking at her. "I know it's hard for her to admit when she needs a shoulder to lean on."

"Thanks, man."

Elias left them alone and as soon as he was out of sight Ava punched Derek in the arm.

"Jerk!"

"Why are you hitting me? I'm giving up my evening to spend time with a lonely old spinster."

"Ass." She swung with her other hand, and he grabbed that wrist before she could connect.

"Oh, an angry, lonely old spinster."

"I hate you." She struggled to free herself, but he was too strong, and he brought her closer so that her chest came against his.

Her body reacted immediately. Her nipples went tight, and warmth spread through her limbs. She forgot to struggle and let herself rest against him.

"You're going to feel bad about telling me you hate me. What do you want for dinner?"

"You roasting over an open fire."

"What's with you and fire all the time? I'm starting to worry about you. I think you really might be a pyromaniac."

"Get off me," she said, not making any attempt to pull herself away from him. He felt too good, and frankly it was nice just to lean against someone so strong.

"Only if you kiss me."

"No. I find you repulsive."

"So? Do it anyway."

He took his hands off her wrists and ran his large hands down her back. It was a soothing touch, and it caused her to wrap her arms around him in an almost an involuntary move. This closeness was clearly something her body wanted, even though her brain was screaming out that this was wrong.

"Let's be nice to each other for a moment. I saw a delivery truck pull in this morning as I was leaving. What was it this time?"

"A diamond necklace, a matching bracelet and roses, lots and lots of roses."

"He's trying to wear you down."

"I know. He has excellent taste in jewelry."

"Please tell me you're not tempted."

"I'm not. I'm going to go on a hunt for another rich man soon. This time I'll find one in his eighties and earn the money the old-fashioned way—inherit it when he dies."

"Don't say things like that," he said softly, but seriously.

"I'm too mean to find a husband. I'll die a mean, old, lonely spinster."

His eyes swept across her face. "Men would kill for the chance to be with you. When you are ready, love will find you."

Her heart squeezed. He was looking at her with tenderness in his pretty blue eyes. "Damn it, Derek. I don't like it when you're nice to me." She stood on her tiptoes and gave him the kiss that he had asked for earlier and then one more that was a little longer because it felt so good the first time.

"Go home." She gave him a push, still confused as to why she wanted to be so close to him when she was still so heartsore.

"I'm coming back for dinner. There's a Caribbean fusion joint in town that makes great mango chicken. I'll pick up some beef patties, too."

She wanted to tell him not to bother, but again she couldn't seem to make herself do so. "Get more wine. And ice cream. Elias loves mint chocolate chip."

## Chapter 7

Derek walked into his aunt Clara's kitchen the next evening and was greeted by the smell of his grandmother's famous chicken stew. Nanny sat at the table rolling biscuits, while his aunt was at the stove adding something to the large cast-iron pot.

"Well, look at what the cat dragged in." His grandmother looked at him with a raised white brow.

"Hello, Nanny. How are you?"

"Wasting away," she said dramatically. "My favorite grandson doesn't visit me as often as he used to, and it's breaking my heart."

"You want me to call him?" Derek asked as he took the chair beside her. "Kev is in high school now, Nanny. He's not going to have time for you like he used to."

An amused sparkling came into her eyes. "Fresh, boy."

"Hello, Aunt Clara. Are you upset with me, too?"

"Of course not. You can do no wrong in my eyes. You're perfect. But if you could find time in your busy schedule to see your widowed aunt at least once a week, I'd find you even more perfect." She winked at him.

"We know you're busy, Derek," Nanny said. "We're just used to seeing you around more. Maybe your special lady friend is taking up most of your time?"

"Special lady friend?"

"Your mother told me that she saw you at Hack's with a woman."

"That was Ava." He shook his head. "She told you about that? Did she also tell you what she was up to that evening?"

He wasn't surprised that the news that he was with Ava had gotten back to his family. All eyes were on him wherever he went. He was just surprised that his mother was the one to tell them.

"I'm sure she wasn't there alone," Nanny said with a grimace. "Who's Ava?"

"Ava Bradley. She's renting the house next door to me."

"The girl who called off the wedding of the century?" his aunt asked.

"Yes. She's having a hard time. Her fiancé broke her heart."

"She found out he was cheating on her." Nanny nodded. "He looks like the type."

"It's more than that. It's a much bigger betrayal. I took her to Hack's to cheer her up."

And because he wanted to be with her. Just like last night. He hadn't planned to go over there, thinking that if he kept his distance, he wouldn't be so enthralled with her. But then he saw her Hula-Hooping and laughing with such unguarded joy that he couldn't help but walk over to her. He didn't care that she was with her brother. His body needed to be near hers.

And then she had kissed him. Two sweet, soft kisses, like the kind two longtime lovers would share. He should have gone home after that and stayed there because he knew the more time he spent with her, the more he would want her. But he couldn't stay home.

He had returned to her with dinner and drinks and stayed the entire evening. Elias had joined them when he woke up, and they continued to have a good time. He liked seeing Ava and her twin together. On the surface she didn't seem like a very loving person, but Derek could tell by the way she interacted with her brother that she loved very deeply. It was probably why she was so blown away by her breakup. She had wasted all that love on someone who was unworthy. He wondered what it would feel like to be on the receiving end of all that unfiltered love.

It might be life altering.

"So there's nothing going on between you two?" His grandmother couldn't hide the disappointment in her voice.

"No, ma'am. Vermeulen did a number on her. And he is still trying to get her back. He keeps sending her astronomically expensive jewelry."

"Do you think she'll go back? It's hard to say no to being a billionaire's wife," Nanny said.

"I don't think she'll go back. She actually loved him for him and not his money."

"Which is why he wants her back," Aunt Clara said with a nod. "Isn't this the same woman you called a gold-digging ice goddess last year when the resort debacle was at its peak?"

"It wasn't one of my finer moments."

"You're a good boy to spend time with her. I know heart-broken women give you the hives," his aunt said.

"After dealing with your mother's many heartbreaks over the years, I thought you'd rather have your teeth pulled with a pair of rusty pliers rather than deal with that again."

"Ava's not my mother," he said. The more he got to know her, the more he was realizing that.

\* \* \*

A couple of days later Ava walked into Derek's house after knocking for some time. She knew he was home. His truck was in the driveway. As she entered his house, she heard the whine of an electric saw.

His place was an absolute disaster. It was clear that he used the first floor of his home as a workshop. There was furniture everywhere, and not his personal furniture but the pieces he was in the stages of making. Her eyes immediately went to the large whiskey-barrel coffee table in the center of the room. It was made from reclaimed wood, and it was rustic and gorgeous and something she had never seen before. There were benches and bookshelves, TV consoles and kitchen tables. She had wondered why a single man had needed a house so large, and she now understood why. He needed the space for his art. His furniture was art. She had seen some of his pieces at Carlos's house, and somewhere in the back of her mind she knew that he had made them. Now that she got the chance to study them up close, she could see just how exquisite they were.

She was growing annoyed with Derek again. It wasn't fair that he seemed to be good at so many things when she wasn't sure she was good at even one thing. She had been feeling restless this morning. She was done with her deep mourning over the loss of her future with Max. Now it was time for her to do something with her life. But what?

There was a desk in the corner of the room with a computer on it and a slew of unorganized papers. She walked over to it, just with the intention of straightening things a bit. She was a neat person by nature, and as she started to straighten she began to sort the mess into piles. Receipts. Emails from customers. Invoices.

After they were put in the proper places, she spotted a clean rag and began to dust his desk and his computer screen. When that was done, she went around the room collecting all the tools that were lying around and put them in the large toolbox near the door. There were a few mugs around, and she placed them in the kitchen sink. Seeing that there were even more mugs in there, she decided to give them all a good scrubbing. And when that was done, she decided to give the entire kitchen a good scrubbing.

She had half her body in the refrigerator, scraping dried jelly off the shelf, when he walked into the room.

"People break into houses for lots of reasons, but I don't think cleaning them is one of those reasons."

"Um… I'm sorry." She stood up and faced him. Her heart immediately beat a little faster, and it wasn't because she had been busted. He looked damn good today, wearing work gloves and a sawdust-covered shirt. He was just so big. And even though he was a few feet away from her, she could feel the heat roll off him. He was so different from Max, who was finer boned and the height of male elegance.

Derek was incredibly masculine and strong. He could pick her up and toss her over his shoulder, and something about that appealed to her.

"I know I shouldn't have walked into your house and started cleaning, but I knocked and you didn't answer. I just meant to straighten up a little, but I got carried away."

He just cocked his head to the side and looked at her.

"I was feeling restless," she explained.

"I can tell." He took his gloves off, tossed them on the counter and came toward her. "You just can't come into a man's home and be bent over in his refrigerator without some consequences."

"Consequences?" She swallowed hard. "How about a thank you, you big jerk? Your house is a disaster, and I've been working my fingers to the bone to make it habitable."

"Oh, poor princess. Had to do some actual work and now she's all worn out." He placed his big, hot hands around her waist, and she couldn't think clearly.

"Shut up, Derek."

"Okay." He placed his mouth over hers and gave her a shockingly sexual kiss. And what was even more shocking was that she let him. She wrapped her arms around him and kissed him back. It wasn't something she could control anymore.

He smelled like aftershave and wood, and his body was so…solid. And despite what she told him, he was a phenomenal kisser. He made her mind turn to mush as his tongue swept inside her mouth. His hands slid down her back to her behind, and he cupped her flesh, squeezing it between his fingers and taking her beyond just being turned on. She could feel the wetness forming between her legs. It had always taken her forever to get aroused when Max touched her. And he had always taken the more sensual approach. Every time they were together he had to seduce her with wine and candles and silk sheets. Derek just had to look at her and she melted.

He broke the kiss and slid his lips to her ear. "I know why you are so restless. Your body is craving satisfaction."

"What?" She pulled away from him slightly so that she could look into his eyes.

"You never would have let me kiss you like that unless you needed to be kissed like that."

"I'm not sure what you are talking about. But clearly this was a mistake." She tried to pull away from him but he caught her wrist and kissed her again.

And damn it, she kissed him back.

"See?" He gave her a smug smile. "When is the last time you had a really good orgasm?"

She opened her mouth to chastise him, but no words came out because she couldn't think of the last time she'd had a really good orgasm. The last few times she had had sex she wasn't able to have one, not that Max had noticed.

They weren't intimate often. Now it made sense. He had been sleeping with his mistress the entire time.

"I can do that for you."

"I don't want to have sex with you," she said firmly, but she knew she was lying. Mentally she didn't want to sleep with him. It was too soon after her breakup. She was still too messed up, but her body wanted him. It craved his touch. She had spent the evening with him when Elias was over. All night Derek gave her tiny touches that to anyone else would have seemed innocent. His fingers touched hers every time he handed her something. He sat too close to her on the couch when they were watching that movie. His lips lingered just a little bit too long on her cheek when he kissed her goodbye.

He was causing her to go out of her mind. She wanted him. She wanted to feel good, and he was the only person who could make her feel that way.

"I'm not suggesting sex." He ran his hand over the back of her bare thigh, sliding it under her flowing skirt. He touched her behind again, slipping his fingers into her underwear and feeling the skin no one had seen in such a long time. "Let me touch you. I promise you'll feel better."

She nodded. She couldn't manage any words in that moment. Things had escalated so quickly, and she didn't want to give herself any time to think, to back out. She believed Derek. She believed he would make her feel good.

His hands went up her shirt to unhook her bra. He didn't remove it, just loosened it enough so that he could place his hand on her breast. His thumb stroked her very tight nipple, and his eyes flicked up to hers. There was such arousal in them. It was the same look she'd seen flash in his eyes when she was Hula-Hooping. Every woman should have a man look at them with such desire at least once in their lives.

He kissed her again. She shut her eyes, letting him kiss her as deeply as he wanted. She couldn't move; she couldn't even kiss him back this time because she was feeling too many things.

And when his hands hiked up her skirt and pulled down her underwear, her knees almost gave way. She was throbbing now. She couldn't remember ever being this aroused.

He put his hand between her legs, running his thick middle finger over her lips. He froze.

"You're so wet." His voice came out in a rasp. His chest heaved. In one quick move he bent to remove her flip-flops and her underwear, which pooled at her ankles; then he took her hand, pulling her out of the room. She was expecting to go to his upstairs bedroom. She told him she didn't want to have sex, but she was going to let him do whatever he wanted with her body because she knew it would be good.

But he didn't take her to his room. He took her to his den, which had a couch, a television and a wall of bookshelves. He pushed her down on the couch before going to his knees, his upper body settling between her legs.

She wasn't sure what he was going to do, but for some reason she wasn't expecting what he did. He opened her and gifted her with one long, firm lick that made her entire body tremble. "Oh God, Derek."

"You're so sweet," he told her before he licked the length of her again. He was definitely a man who knew what he was doing, who enjoyed what he was doing. He gave her slow, intimate kisses there, like she was the most precious thing in the world, and then sucked her most sensitive part into his mouth. She cried out, saying words she wasn't sure made sense, but she couldn't control it and just when she thought she couldn't feel anymore he slipped two fingers inside her.

She swore as he began to pump his fingers and work his tongue in unison. She didn't feel like herself. She had never felt this free with a man. It was Derek. He made her uncomfortable. He made her angry. He made her want to be near him. It was hard to explain why.

Orgasm took over her entire body. Sex had always been pleasant, and she had looked forward more to the closeness of the process than the end result, but not today. There was no pleasantness here. She felt raw and stripped and amazing. What Derek did to her left her completely breathless and boneless.

This was an experience.

"Derek." She panted. He must have known that she wanted him with her because he covered her body with his own and lay on top of her. She wrapped her arms around him, loving the way his heavy body on top of her felt, loving the way he smelled like her and wood and aftershave.

She could have stayed there forever like that, but he kissed her neck and climbed off her. "I've got to get back to work. You feel better? If not, my personal bathroom could use a deep cleaning."

He walked out then, and she swore again. That man would make her pull her hair out.

## Chapter 8

A few evenings later, Derek stepped outside on his porch. He rarely was in a bad mood, but today had caught up with him and he'd found himself being irrationally annoyed all afternoon. Being outside made him feel slightly better. The sun was going to set soon, painting the sky a gorgeous salmon-orange color. There was a breeze blowing, causing the leaves on the trees around him to gently swish. He looked toward the ocean in the distance, and it reminded him of the last time he was at the beach. He was with Ava in his truck, eating cake as the sun set.

And just as if he'd magically conjured her, he spotted her walking up the road. She was in a black two-piece that was sexy but understated. Her hair was pinned up. Her look was almost old-fashioned, like she was a throwback to another time. She looked just like a pinup. He couldn't take his eyes off her.

She must have felt his gaze, and she looked up at him,

giving him a little wave as she walked past his house. He couldn't let that be the only interaction they had that day.

He stepped off his porch and met her as she turned into her driveway.

"Invite me inside," he said to her.

"What if I don't want to be bothered with you today?"

"You like Thai food?"

She paused before she answered. "Yes."

"I'll buy you dinner."

"Do I have to put on actual clothes for this dinner?"

"I would very much like to see you eat dinner naked, but I would be afraid to see what happened if you spilled soup on yourself."

She frowned at him. "You know what I meant. Are you having it delivered?"

"Yes."

"Are you flirting with me?"

"Yes."

She cocked her head to the side and looked at him. "Why?"

That was a good question. He didn't know why. He didn't know why he liked her or why she had buried herself so deeply under his skin or why she popped into his head a million times a day. "Something to do." He shrugged.

"Come in." She opened her door, which was unlocked.

"You shouldn't leave your door unlocked like that."

"Why not? Are you saying your island isn't safe, Mr. Mayor?"

"No."

"Don't you leave your door unlocked?"

"Yes, and you broke in, which is exactly my point! Any old thing could just walk in off the street."

She rolled her eyes. "There's about a quarter of a mile between me and the next neighbor, so I'm assuming you're worried about you breaking in here? What are you going to do? Build me a new patio set when I'm out shopping? Actually, I think I would like that. Can you do that for me?"

He followed her inside the house, trying not to focus on the way her behind swished as she walked. "You want some of my furniture?"

"It's very beautiful, Derek," she said with no sign of snark. "Although I don't know where I'd put it. This place is furnished, and I currently don't have anywhere else to go."

"I thought you had a condo in Miami."

"I'm renting it out. My tenant signed a two-year lease. I thought I'd be married and living in Europe by now."

He could hear the tinge of sadness in her voice. It had been almost a month now. In the big scheme of things it was only a short time, but he hated that she was still mourning the loss of such a big creep. He didn't want her to be sad about it anymore.

"I could make you something small. Not furniture."

"Like what? A trinket box? For all the jewelry my ex keeps sending me?"

"You got more?"

She nodded. "Black diamonds. Absolutely gorgeous. I sent them back. What else can you make me?"

"A dollhouse. My uncle was an architect, and he used to build my cousin elaborate dollhouses with furniture and working lights. He showed me how. That's how I got into woodworking. I can make just about anything."

"Make me something. Anything. Surprise me."

"That's going to cost you. A lot."

"I have to spend time with you. I think that's payment enough."

"Have to? I'm the mayor of this island. Everyone wants me at their events. You should be thrilled to be honored by my presence."

"If everyone wants you at their events, why are you in my house?"

"Maybe I don't want to go to a place where I'm treated kindly and respected. Maybe I'm a glutton for punishment."

Ava stepped forward and placed her hand on his cheek. "What's the matter, Derek?" she asked softly.

"Huh?"

She touched his chest, her hand resting on his heart. "There's a little edge to you today. And the fact that you sought me out after not speaking to me for days is telling. You want to distract yourself from something."

"Maybe it's because I find you incredibly beautiful and I want to be near you."

"Maybe you're full of crap." She grinned at him. "Order our dinner. I'm going to go change."

"Don't."

"Don't?"

It was an outrageous request on his part. He couldn't really expect her to eat dinner in her bathing suit, but he liked the way she looked in it. He wanted to dine with a pinup girl tonight.

"No. Keep it on."

He thought she was going to protest, but she just nodded and set her beach bag down before she handed him the phone. "I want pad thai."

They ate dinner sitting on the couch that night, watching television, talking during commercial breaks. Derek sat close to her, his warm body pressed against hers. It was a comfortable evening. He was one of the few people she could just be quiet with. For once in her life she didn't have to worry about impressing anyone.

"My mother called today," he told her when the show ended. "That's why I'm feeling funky."

"You two treated each other like acquaintances. You're not close?"

"I spent more time with my aunt and uncle than I ever

did with her. They would have liked to have raised me full-time, but my mother refused to turn over custody. I was never sure why she didn't."

"You're speaking as if she doesn't love you."

He shrugged, which wasn't what she was expecting. She had seen the tension between them. Anita was the opposite of her mother, who would kiss the skin off your face if you let her. If there was one thing Ava was sure of in her life, it was that she was loved deeply. Derek was loved, too. Hideaway Island adored him, but that kind of love was surface love. He needed to be loved deeply. Everyone deserved that.

"What did she want?"

"For me to fix something."

"And that's the only reason she ever calls, right? When she wants something?"

"Yeah…" He shook his head. "I shouldn't have brought it up. I'm sorry. I sound like a whiny little punk."

"I would tell you if you did." She smiled at him. "Tell me about your mother." She placed her hand on his hard thigh. It suddenly made her think about the other day. After he had finished giving her the best orgasm of her life he had laid his big, hard body on top of hers. She loved the feel of him; even sitting this close to her was giving her a little charge.

He had walked away from her that afternoon, lying on his couch with her skirt up and her legs open. It left her feeling incredibly vulnerable. She didn't know what she had been expecting from him, but she hadn't expected that. She had taken a hard blow from Max. She never wanted to be put in that position with a man again, but Derek had come along quite unexpectedly, and she was starting to like him. She just needed to keep herself from liking him too much.

She definitely needed to keep some space between them, but right now she couldn't make herself move away.

He touched her hand, absently rubbing his thumb over her now-bare ring finger. "I'm the product of an affair my mother had with a married man. On an island this small you would think everyone would know that, but they don't. My mother and my grandmother had big falling-out over it and my mother moved off-island. She moved back when I was two."

"She broke things off with your father?"

"No. She was his mistress until I was ten. But he wasn't a hands-on father. Moving us closer to her family gave her the freedom to chase my father. She thought she would force him to leave his wife if she had me. She thought that we would be one big happy family. The plan backfired. A young, hot mistress becomes less appealing when she has a rowdy toddler to chase around."

"How is your relationship with your father?"

"Nearly nonexistent. My choice. Not his."

"Why?"

"It's hard to explain. I look like him. More than any of his other legitimate children, and he's strangely proud of that. When I got a little older he used to summon me to his office in Miami and tell me all about his business and how to run it and how to get what I wanted out of life."

"He was grooming you to take over."

"Yes. He never tried to hide the fact. Everyone knew I was his son. Including his oldest son, who he called into the office just before I was going away to college. He humiliated him that day, telling him that he was weak, and because of that he would have no hope of becoming a great man and that he was going to leave everything to me if my brother didn't shape up. He did it right in front of me. I lost it that day. I blew up at him. I never went by it, but Bernal was my legal last name. I had it changed. I refused to speak to him. He threatened to cut me off. But I didn't care because I didn't want any of his money. I took out loans and worked my way through college woodworking."

"Bernal? Your father isn't Victor Bernal, is he?"

He nodded. "You know him?"

"He's one of the richest men in the country. He and Max play golf together."

"And now you know why I hated your fiancé so much."

"Oh, lord." She rubbed her forehead. "They are two of a kind, aren't they? You must think I'm like your mother."

His eyes went wide. "Why do you say that?"

"Young woman gives up nearly everything to be with a rich older man."

"But you were going to be the wife. My mother was always just going to be the woman on the side."

"And neither one of us could stand the roles we were in. She didn't want to be the mistress, and I didn't want to be the wife."

"What do you mean you didn't want to be his wife? You were days from walking down the aisle."

"It didn't feel right," she admitted to him. "I didn't feel like I could be who I really was with him."

"Who are you?"

"I don't know. That's why I'm here, trying to figure it out. But we're talking about your messed-up life right now. Not mine."

"My life isn't so messed up. My parents are the only two people in the world who get to me."

"Hey, I thought I got under your skin."

"You do." He said, picking up her hand and locking his fingers with hers. "But in a very different way."

She didn't know what to say to that, but she found herself leaning over to kiss the side of his face. He slid his hands up her neck and cupped her jaw, looking into her eyes for a long moment before he kissed her.

It was one of those kisses that robbed her of her breath, that made her feel like she was having an out-of-body experience. He didn't let up. He just kept kissing her and kissing her until she couldn't support her own weight. She would have let him kiss her like that forever, but he broke the kiss.

"Damn you, Derek. Damn you for doing that to me."

"Damn you for making me want to do that."

She slipped her hand up his shirt to feel his hard stomach. He sucked in a breath. "If you touch me like that, this is going to escalate, and I'm not sure you're ready for that."

"Well, I do owe you a favor."

"A favor?" He frowned.

"Like the one you did for me at your house the other day."

"Oh," he said, nodding very slowly. "Can I choose how you're going to repay me?"

She nodded, feeling excitement build in her chest. "I can always say no."

"Of course. Will you take this off for me?" He touched the top of her bathing suit. He didn't want her to change out of it when she got home. She'd put on weight since she had been here. Her entire family had told her that she was too thin before her wedding. The closer she got to the event, the less she recognized herself. She had morphed into another woman, and now she was changing again and she still wasn't comfortable in her body. But tonight she had noticed the way Derek had looked at her. Lingering, hot looks that made her feel incredible. She got tingles every time she had caught him staring.

"Yes." She stood up and tugged at the tie that held up the bathing suit. She didn't take her eyes off him as she slowly removed it. There was hunger there and as much as watching him look at her turned her on, she also felt incredibly stupid all over again. The man she was about to spend the rest of her life with had never looked at her with this much desire.

"Will you take off the bottoms, too?" he asked her as he stood up. She nodded again and removed them. She was completely exposed to him, completely vulnerable again, which she hated. She had never been this kind of woman. She didn't strip for men she wasn't in a long-term relationship with. But it was kind of freeing, because there were dozens of things that she had done with Derek that she would never have imagined doing with another person. She wasn't exactly sure who she was, but she felt like she could be herself with him.

She was sure he was going to approach her when he got up, but he walked to the door, picking up the Hula-Hoop that was beside it.

"What are you doing with that?"

"I think we both know what I want you to do with this?"

"Put it around your neck to see if I can choke you with it?"

He gave her a devastatingly wicked grin. "I'm not into that. I saw you Hula-hooping that day and ever since then I been imagining how you would look doing it naked."

She took it from him. "This is what you want?"

"Very much."

"Okay. Go sit down."

He did as she ordered leaning back on the couch, his hands tucked behind his head and looked up at her with anticipation. This was a situation that she never thought she would be in, but as odd as it was, she found herself okay with it. She knew Derek was a busy man, but when he was with her, she had all his attention. He didn't have his phone with him tonight. It was nice to be with someone who wasn't constantly staring at a screen or waiting for the next big deal.

She started to Hula-Hoop, not sure if there was a seductive way to do it, but she kept going. Derek grinned at her, and then his grin turned into full-blown laughter. It stung. She dropped the Hula-Hoop.

"You are such an incredible asshole. Get out!" She

started for her bedroom, but he grabbed her wrist and tumbled her into his lap.

"Wait. No. You're upset."

"Of course I'm upset. I take my clothes off for you, and you're laughing at me. I haven't been feeling too great about myself, and you laugh at me when I am literally the most exposed I have ever been."

"No, baby." The concern on his face was clear. "You think I was laughing at the way you look? Are you insane?" He cupped her bottom in his hand. "And what kind of man do you think I am? Do you really think I would do something like that to hurt you?"

She thought about it for a moment. He wasn't that kind of man. The hot looks he had been giving her all night weren't a figment of her imagination. "No woman likes to hear laughing when she takes off her clothes."

"Point taken. I'm sorry, Ava."

"Why were you laughing?"

"I just cannot believe any of this. Five weeks ago I couldn't stand the sight of you, and now we're here. It's surreal. I can't believe you actually did this for me." He pulled her closer and wrapped his arms tightly around her. "You're sweet. You hide it under your perfect beauty, but you are very sweet. And very sensitive."

"I'm a mess," she whispered. "And you're the only one I'm allowing to see that."

"You're the only one outside of my family who knows about my father. We're even." He took a deep breath. "It bothers me that you think I would hurt you like that."

"You walked away from me the other day. You left me exposed and walked out of the room, telling me some crap about your bathroom. I wasn't sure what to think."

"You told me that you didn't want to have sex, and I knew that if I was around you any longer, I would have broken." He placed his lips on her ear and spoke into it. "I left you and went straight to my bedroom to take care of myself. I have never been so hard in my life. And every day since then, I think about the way you looked and sounded and tasted and I get hard all over again. I feel like a damn teenage boy again, touching myself as I think about you."

He was arousing her with his words, but even if he had been completely silent in that moment, she still would have felt the rush and the throb between her legs. She liked the feel of his arms wrapped around her. She liked the way he had stroked down her bare back. She had never experienced this closeness with anyone before. It was intoxicating, and it was happening at the wrong time in her life.

She didn't know what was going to between them, but she was feeling entirely too much for this man when she had been prepared to marry another just a short while ago. "Let me touch you," she said to him.

"Not as a favor."

"What?" She looked into his eyes.

"Touch me because you want to touch me, because it will make you feel good. That's why I touched you. Don't do it because you feel like you owe me something."

"I want to." She shifted herself in his lap and ran her hand down his thick erection that was covered by his jeans. "I wanted to that day. You should have stayed."

"You're going through a lot right now, and I don't want you to look back on this and feel like I was taking advantage of you. That is the last thing I would ever do."

"I know. You're annoyingly noble. I won't feel used. I am going through something right now, and I want to feel good. You make me feel good."

He closed the distance between their mouths and gave her one of those long, slow kisses and made her feel like she was floating.

"Just because I let you kiss me like that doesn't mean I like it or you."

"Yeah." He kissed her again. "I'm gross, and so are my kisses."

"Uh-huh." She unbuttoned his jeans and slid her hand inside of them. He was hard and hot and smooth, and a million dirty thoughts ran through her mind in that moment. There were so many ways she could please him. She could kiss him, lick him, suck him into her warm, wet mouth. Or she could rise over him and slid herself all the way down until he filled her up.

"Slow down, baby. You're too good at that." She had taken him from his pants and was stroking him. She hadn't realized; she was that lost in her thoughts of him. "I want to touch you, too," he groaned and rolled them on to the couch so that they were on their sides.

He placed his hands between her legs, finding her slick with desire. She was close to coming, and he hadn't even touched her; touching him was enough.

He gave her a hot openmouthed kiss as he stroked her. She was a grown woman. She had been with men before. She wasn't even having sex with Derek, but this was one of the most erotic experiences of her life. She was completely naked, he was fully dressed and the way the rough fabric of his clothing felt on her smooth skin was delicious. There may have been that barrier between him, but she felt so close to him.

Her climax was building quickly, and so she stroked him faster, squeezing her hand around him tighter. She loved the guttural noises he made. She loved that she was making him feel good. She knew it wasn't going to be the last time she they were like this. Whatever was going on between them was addictive.

"I can't hold on anymore, Ava. I need you to come now." She wanted this to go on forever, but she knew he was losing control so she moved against his hand, taking herself over the edge. As soon as the waves started to overtake her, she heard him cry out and shudder against her. They lay there breathless for a moment, chests heaving, satisfaction snaking over them. He started to kiss her. Little kisses up the side of her face.

"Stay here." He got up and walked toward the back of the house. He returned a few minutes later with a washcloth and her bathrobe. He gently cleaned her off and helped her into her robe before he took her into his arms again. He kissed her hair, and she found the moment so sweet, so thoughtful that she was growing emotional. She wanted to be with him again; she didn't want this night to end.

It was too much. She could let herself feel good, but she couldn't get attached. Not right now.

She softly kissed his mouth and stood up. "Go home, Mr. Mayor."

"What?" He looked bewildered.

"Get out. Go home. I have things to do."

"Like what? Retile your bathroom?"

"The backsplash in the kitchen. I'll see you around."

"You're really kicking me out?"

"Yup."

"Just like that?"

She held up a peace sign, which caused him to grin. It was one of those devastating, wickedly sexy smiles that made her insides go all gooey. It was the exact reason he needed to go. She couldn't bear to tell him to leave again, so she walked out of the room, knowing that she was going to spend the rest of her night thinking about him.

## Chapter 9

Derek turned the knob on Ava's front door and let himself into her house the next morning. Their wineglasses were still on the table from the night before and he suspected that she had gone directly to bed when she had sent him away.

He didn't like being sent away. He didn't know what the hell was going on between them. Friends with benefits seemed too seedy, too disrespectful even though that's how he would characterize most of his relationships over the past ten years or so. He liked Ava. He could talk to Ava. He wanted to be near Ava and a big part of him wanted to protect her. It was an odd feeling, one he had never had before, but he wanted to keep her safe. She had been hurt and was still so certain that someone was going to hurt her again. It was the next morning, and he was still bothered by the fact that she thought he would hurt her, humiliate her for his pleasure.

But that's what it must have been like when she learned that Max had a mistress and three children that surely others must have known about. It had to have been a brutal blow, but not all men were like that. He wanted to show her that some could be trusted.

He walked into her bedroom, finding her asleep and looking nearly angelic with the blankets wrapped around her. He climbed into bed next to her, internally sighing when her curvy, warm body inched closer to his.

"If your dirty shoes are in my bed, I'm going to punch you," she said without opening her eyes or moving.

He sat up, took them off and returned to her. She hadn't kicked him out or screamed. She had automatically known it was him.

"You should have locked your door. I could have been some stranger here to do bad things to you."

She opened her eyes and glanced at the clock on the nightstand. "It's 7:02 a.m. Anyone who comes to your house before eight without coffee is clearly up to no good. What do you want, Derek?"

He ran his lips across the skin of her neck. She smelled amazing, some sort of indescribable combination of woodsy and citrus that turned him on. He wanted to roll her over and make love to her until they were both limp and incoherent, but that really wasn't the reason he'd come by this morning. "Are you busy today?"

"Yes, incredibly busy. I have three court shows to watch and then my stories come on at one and I'm pretty much slammed till four."

"I need your help. I have to ship about a dozen pieces out today, and run a bunch of mayor-related errands. And you're the most organized person I know."

"You don't even know me that well."

"You organized my orders by type of piece, price and date of order. I've never seen anything so efficient. I need that in my life."

She gifted him with a beautiful, sleepy smile. "No one

appreciates my skills. Elias says he finds my constant need to organize very annoying."

"I appreciate it. Come help me today."

"What's in it for me? You want me to spend the whole day working? I thought you thought I was a fairly useless woman, and my only purpose was to look good on the arm of a man."

"No. You're good at cleaning. More women should be like that."

Her face went outraged and she punched his upper arm.

"You hit hard."

"You're a jerk."

"I was joking." He bent to kiss her cheek. "Help me today, princess. It will make you feel good to know that you are helping out a friend."

"But this bed is so warm." She moaned and rolled onto her back. "And my eyes are so heavy. I'm not sure I have the energy to get up."

She was going to get up and help him. He knew that she was just busting his chops, and now she was teasing him. She was braless and her nightie was dangerously low-cut. The tops of her breasts looked lovely in the morning light. They were distracting the hell out of him. He ran his knuckles over her cleavage. Her skin was buttery soft, and the touch brought him back to last night when he'd held her naked body in his arms.

"Oh, Derek. Don't start with me this morning."

"What are you talking about?" He tugged at the bodice of her nightgown a little, just enough to reveal one of her breasts. "We're just talking." He blew on her nipple, causing it to pebble immediately. "I heard the weather is going to be nice today." He lowered his mouth and flicked his tongue across her.

She made the best little noise from her throat. He wanted to hear more of that. He loved the little noises she made, how responsive she was. He ran his tongue around her areola before he took it completely into his mouth. He knew he was arousing her and in turn arousing himself. If he allowed himself, he could be here all day.

But he really hadn't come here to do this. Still, he couldn't leave until he knew she was satisfied. He hiked up her nightgown only to find that she wasn't wearing any underwear. He had to bite his lip to keep himself from groaning.

Moisture had already formed between her legs, and he wanted to tease her, see how wild he could make her before he touched her, but he didn't play around today. He covered her mouth with his lips and kissed her as he rubbed her in slow, firm circles. Her orgasm was quick and hot and intense.

"Get dressed and meet me at my house in fifteen minutes," he said after she recovered.

"And if I don't?"

"I'm coming back here and we're going to repeat this process all over again."

"And how is that supposed to motivate me to get out of this bed?"

"Ava…" He shook his head and dropped a kiss on the side of her neck. "You drive me absolutely crazy."

"And yet you haven't tried to sleep with me yet."

"I want to. But you're not ready yet."

"I think we both know that whenever you touch me I become ready ridiculously fast. I don't think I could turn you away."

"I'm not going to seduce you. You'll come to me when you're ready."

"How long will you wait?"

"As long as it takes." He got up and put his shoes back on. "My house. Fifteen minutes. I'll have coffee for you."

* * *

A few hours later Ava was sitting cross-legged on the floor of Derek's living room turned workshop. She was sanding a side table. And while she never thought she would be sanding anything, she was actually enjoying herself. They had gotten a lot done that morning. They packed up all the pieces that needed to be shipped out. She organized his computer files and showed him an easier way to keep his books. They worked surprisingly well together, despite the fact that every time he looked at her a whole herd of butterflies went wild in her stomach. She had to stop letting him touch her. She had gone to bed that night promising herself that she was going to put some distance between them, just so she could clear her head and figure out what the hell she was going to do with her life. She still had no idea, and Derek was further complicating things.

His visit this morning had been unexpected but welcome. She could have stopped him from taking her nipple into his mouth. She could have stopped him from slipping his hand between her legs and bringing her a quick and intense orgasm, but she didn't. Because she had wanted it to happen.

She wished it could be just sex, that she could be one of those women who could have just a physical relationship with a man, but Derek was really becoming her friend, probably the best friend she'd had in a long time. She loved her sister-in-law, but Virginia was family. She could just talk to Derek. She couldn't talk to anyone else like that.

"You're doing good work." He took the sandpaper from her and pulled her to her feet. "I'm surprised you haven't gone screaming from the house."

"I've gotten used to your ugly face by now. Why would I do that?"

"Your nails." He studied her fingers. "You seem like

one of those women who would faint if her manicure got messed up."

"I wonder how the people of Hideaway Island would react if they knew how you really were?"

"They'll never know." He swiftly kissed her mouth. "You're the only one who brings it out in me. Come with me, I have to do some mayor stuff in town today."

"Okay. Let me change."

"Why?" He frowned at her before leading her to his truck. "You're gorgeous. I think you wore that dress to drive to me to distraction."

She was wearing a peach-colored knit dress that she had gotten off the clearance rack in town. She wore no makeup and cheap earrings. A few months ago, she would never have gone to her mailbox without eyeliner; now she was going out into the world with a bare face. She felt a little naked, but it was freeing. She had always been so scared of what the world thought of her. For the past few years she had been so wrapped up in being Max's perfect fiancée, she had forgotten to be herself; she had forgotten who she really was.

Derek squeezed her hand, causing her to look up at him. They were holding hands. She hadn't noticed. It shouldn't seem like such a natural thing to do and yet it was.

"What are you thinking about?"

"About how my life and how things went terribly wrong."

"Terribly wrong? You're about to ride around the most beautiful island in the world with me. I would think that you must have done something in a past life that let you earn this moment."

"Yes, I'm about to get in a pickup truck that was probably built the year my great-grandmother was born, with a man who insults me, instead of traveling on a private jet and shopping in Europe with my billionaire husband. Lucky me."

"Yes. Lucky you. Private jets are pretentious. But seriously, what *are* you going to do with your life now?"

"I already told you. Find me another rich man," she blurted out because he was still holding her hand and looking at her in that concerned way that made her chest feel funny. She didn't want to be serious with him right now. They told each other things they had never spoken aloud to anyone else, and it was bringing them closer. Each time they were together they got closer, and it made her uncomfortable because she didn't want to get used to this. Hideaway Island couldn't be permanent for her. Eventually she would move on, she would move away from here, she would leave him.

He should just be a pleasant memory. Nothing more.

"I have money. You planning on sinking your hooks into me?"

"It depends…how rich are you?"

"Rich enough to buy you all the takeout you want for the rest of your life. I'm talking all the pizza, tacos and fried seafood your heart desires. Stick with me, baby, and I'll show you how to live."

He made her laugh. It was why she was with him here now. It was why she was going to have a hard time keeping herself closed off to him.

"The more meals I eat with you, the bigger my behind gets."

"My evil little plan is working. Get in the truck. I'm still deciding what I'm going to feed you next."

Derek took her the scenic route around the island, driving with his windows down so that the warm ocean air could come in. He stopped every so often like he was on his rounds. The local bakery, a coffee shop, a little stationery store. He stopped in just to say hello to the owners and invite them to the city hall meetings to voice any concerns. He asked them all to take part in the founder's day celebra-

tions. He shook hands with everyone and seemed genuinely
interested in what they had to say. This was the side of him
she had first encountered, that ultra-good, squeaky-clean
side of him that she had found a little annoying at first.

She knew everyone had to have a dark side, some sort
of secret gain they were after, and Derek did have a darker
side, but he wasn't mayor because he wanted the power.
He just really wanted the best for everyone, which seemed
so opposite of how he should have turned out, according
to his upbringing.

"How are you holding up?" He placed his hand on her
knee as they drove up a road that didn't appear to be open
to the public.

"Why are you asking? Am I being cranky?"

"No. You're being pleasant. I don't trust you when you're
pleasant."

"Do you think I'm one of those women who gets all
nice and quiet when she's upset? You should know from
experience that I get very loud and angry when I'm mad."

"I dragged you out of bed, made you work in my shop
and then dragged you around half the island. Not everyone
can handle my schedule."

"Not everyone gets to have the mayor give them orgasms, either, and I got two in less than twelve hours. Or
am I wrong? Do you give orgasms as frequently as hand-
shakes?"

"Not yet, but if you think it will help me win reelection,
I will." He grinned at her briefly. "I need to stop here for
a minute and say hello."

They pulled up in front of a retirement community,
which had a lovely view of the ocean. If Derek were any
other man, she would think he was only stopping here to
seem like a good guy for the voters, but she had seen him
in action enough today to know that he was coming here,
because it was just what he did.

"This is a very interesting project we have going on here. It's partly residential and privately owned but there is a center here that is free and open to all the seniors on the island."

"It's really beautiful," she said, seeing people stroll along the path that overlooked the ocean. There was a lovely garden filled with lush tropical flowers and a covered courtyard where people were playing card games or just chatting with cool drinks in their hands.

"The restaurant in this place also has the best pot roast I have ever had, but they won't let just anybody eat in there. You have to be accompanied by a senior. I can't wait till I'm sixty." He grinned at her. "I'll finally be able to break my takeout habit. Although I'm sure the delivery drivers of the island would go into mourning over the loss of their tips."

"You'll break your take-out habit before you're sixty," she said as they walked toward the entrance. "Your wife probably won't want to eat out every night."

"My wife? You think I'm going to be getting married?"

"Of course I do. Every single woman in this town has their eye on you. Especially that little bakery owner. I think she's got your spring wedding already planned out in her head."

"That's not true."

"Yes, it is. She gave you her pies."

"So? A lot of the business owners give me their goods. I have had something from practically every business in town at this point."

"But she batted her eyelashes at you and told you that she just didn't give her special pies away to anyone, and that she had been planning a special trip to city hall so she could deliver them to you. I'm seeing a beach wedding. I think a tux isn't the right tone for that wedding."

"I wouldn't get involved with a citizen."

"Why not? It's not against the law."

"I would have to fall in love pretty damn hard to get involved with a woman who lived on the island. I don't want to be involved in any messiness if things don't work out. I am determined to be a scandal-free mayor."

"A breakup doesn't have to be scandalous. Unless you're me. I insist that all my relationships end in a dramatic soap opera fashion."

"I'm not looking to get involved with any of my residents. I love this island. She's who I'm married to."

"I know you love this island, but when you're cold and lonely at night this island can't love you back like a woman could." She paused for a moment and looked up at him. "You're a young, single, sexy man. Who do you go to? I don't believe that you've never slept with anyone from the island."

"We're in public."

"No one can hear me. I'm being quiet. You just don't want to tell me."

"The only woman I can think about getting anything from is you, and it's a huge pain in my ass." He surprised her by kissing her lips. It was an incredibly brief kiss and she could tell it had been impulsive, but he had kissed her in public.

She should be more concerned about it, but at the moment she didn't really care who saw.

## Chapter 10

Derek took Ava's hand and led her inside the senior center until he realized what he was doing. All day he had denied himself. It had just seemed natural to take her hand whenever he was near her. Her fingers just slid so perfectly into his. She was a woman who had just gotten out of a relationship, and he was a man who wasn't looking for any entanglements, but there they were. And he had just kissed her in public, for the entire world to see.

But honestly the kiss didn't matter. He had taken her around town with him. He had introduced her as his friend to everyone they had encountered. It didn't matter if he had never touched her; the fact that they were simply together would get people talking. He hadn't thought about what that might mean for them when he'd asked her to come with him that morning. He just knew that he hadn't gotten enough of her.

She'd sat on the floor with him and sanded a table. She'd lifted and lugged and labeled, and she didn't complain once.

He had been so wrong about her. He felt so incredibly right with her, but it was just the wrong time for it. Plus, he knew her time on this island was limited. She was getting bored here. She was going to move on with her life soon. He knew she was joking when she told him she was going to find herself another rich husband, but it was probably the truth.

Ava was the kind of woman who deserved the best. A successful husband, a life that wasn't this simple. She would be gone before winter, and whatever he was feeling would vanish.

"Is that my long-lost grandson?" He heard his grandmother's voice. "I can't tell. I haven't seen him in ages."

His grandmother was standing just to his left, looking elegant as usual in her designer resort wear. It was hard to believe that his mother came from such a woman. They were polar opposites. "Hello, Nanny. I was hoping to see you here." He walked over and hugged her.

"No. You weren't." She gave the back of his head a small smack. "If you wanted to see me, you would have come to my house. I'm guessing you must have forgotten where it is. You have a GPS on your phone, don't you? I'm sure you can get it to navigate my way."

"I love this woman." Derek heard Ava say. He looked over to see her smiling. Good lord, it knocked him right upside his head every time he saw it. He didn't know how she could be self-conscious about the way she looked. She was the most beautiful woman he had ever seen. He could see a million more women, and his opinion wouldn't change. Naked. Clothed. Face full of makeup or not a stitch on, she was truly one of those rare beauties that he would never tire of seeing.

"I'm sure I would love you, too, dear, if my grandson would introduce us."

"I'm Ava Bradley." She stepped forward and shook her hand. "Derek has decided to be my caretaker this month."

"This is my grandmother, Felicia Patrick," Derek said noticing his grandmother studying her intently. She never missed a thing, and he was wondering what was going through her head in that moment.

"It's lovely to meet you, Mrs. Patrick."

"Call me Nanny. Come sit down and have a chat with me."

"Gladly. I'm living for your ensemble. Your blouse is vintage Ferrara, isn't it? The 1978 collection."

Nanny froze. "How did you know that?"

"I was a fashion buyer. And you're a sample size, aren't you? I bet your closet is amazing."

"Yes, yes, it is." Derek saw excitement in his grandmother's eyes. Ava had just managed to do something that so few people could: win over his grandmother instantly.

Nanny led them to a seat by the window, and the two women launched into a conversation about fashion that Derek didn't understand a word of. He knew that before his grandmother had met his grandfather and settled here, she had led an exciting life. She had modeled all over the world. Spending most of her time in Europe.

"This is such an exquisite ring." Ava took Nanny's hand. "I can't stop looking at it."

"Thank you. It has been in our family for over a hundred years. The Patrick men have proposed with it for the past century. I had all girls and was secretly happy when I did because I'm very attached to it."

"I would be, too." Ava sighed. "If my ex had gotten me something like this, I might have considered going back to him."

"No, you wouldn't have," Derek said.

"I might have. It would have meant that he really knew what I liked, instead of buying me the most expensive thing he could think of. I would have taken it as a sign that he knew the real me."

"But you don't love him. He could give you the world, but I know you wouldn't go back."

"You think you know me so well?" She turned fully in her chair to look at him.

"Not all of you. Not yet. But I'll get there."

And unreadable look flashed in her eyes before she turned back to his grandmother. "Men." She huffed. "Think they know everything."

"I know, dear. Never met a man who didn't think he did." Nanny stood up. "I have a bridge game to get to, but I have loved chatting with you and would very much like to see you again. Come to the house for dinner on Wednesday."

"Nanny, I have a meeting that night," Derek said to her.

"I didn't invite you to come to dinner. I invited Ava," she retorted.

"I'll wait for Derek for dinner, but would you like to go to lunch with me and maybe shopping?"

"That would be wonderful. Let's say the day after tomorrow. We'll meet at eleven thirty in front of Derek's store on Main Street."

"You have a store on Main Street?" Ava's eyes went wide.

"Yes."

"And you choose to keep all that stuff in your home?"

Nanny laughed and walked around the table to hug Ava. "I like you. Keep him on his toes."

"I'm so glad I got to meet you today."

Nanny then came to hug him. "Do not let her go," she said into his ear. He blinked but didn't ask her to clarify, because he knew what she meant and he knew the more time he spent with Ava, the harder it would be to let her go.

The next morning Ava walked over to Derek's house, an open package in her hand. She hadn't planned on seeing him today. She had spent the entire day before with him.

From the moment she got up to the moment she went to bed. She ate her meals with him, did chores with him, worked with him, spent the evening winding down with him, and she never got sick of being with him. She had spent more time with him than she ever had with Max. Even when Max was in town with her. He was always on the phone, always on his laptop, making deals, doing business. Even the night of his proposal he had stepped away to take a call. Derek was present when he was with her. It made her feel special. She was just his neighbor who he had taken under his wing, but she felt important to him.

He would make some woman a wonderful husband.

She opened his door and walked straight inside, knowing that even if she knocked, he wouldn't hear it anyway.

"Derek?" she called out to him.

"Up here." She followed his voice up the stairs to his bedroom, which was the last place she expected him in the middle of a workday. He walked out of his bathroom. He was in his underwear, a pair of black boxer briefs. Her mouth went dry while other parts of her flooded. His body was so beautiful, his legs were muscular, his thighs rock hard and well developed. Every time they were intimate she was the one who had no clothes on while he was fully dressed. She never got to fully appreciate his body, but today she could see it all. He looked good in his clothes, but he looked spectacular without them.

It took a moment before she noticed that he was holding a bloody washcloth to his hand.

"What happened to you?" She dropped what she had been planning to give him on his bed and rushed over to him. She removed the cloth to see that he had sliced all the way across his palm. "We need to go to the hospital. Put on some clothes. I'll drive."

"We do not need to go to the hospital. It's not that deep.

I've cut myself before. It's just one of those things that comes with making furniture for a living."

"It's still bleeding. Did you even clean it well? You probably have tiny little wood splinters in your wound. And bacteria. Your hand is going to fall off and die."

"My hand isn't going to fall off and die."

"Derek, I'm worried. Let me take you to the hospital."

He wrapped his arm around her and kissed the breath out of her. It was the kiss she had wanted all day yesterday but never got. He had just kissed her forehead last night before he left. She hadn't wanted him to leave. She wanted to take him to her bedroom and ask him to stay for the entire night.

But she knew that would be the exact opposite of what she was supposed to be doing. "Yuck," she said when she broke the kiss. "You know that I don't like it when you do that."

"Okay, Ava." He kissed her again, but a little softer this time. She ran her hands up his strong, bare back. She could get addicted to touching him, addicted to the closeness.

"You are just kissing me to distract me from your hand."

"I like that you're worried about me." He cupped her face with his good hand and kissed along her jawline. "It means that you care. It means that you're sweet. It means that you actually like me."

"Shut up. It means I don't want your rotting hand to stink up the neighborhood." She sighed in frustration. "Damn it, Derek. Put on some clothes. How can your body stay hard with all the crap you eat?"

"Why are you so overdressed?" he reached for the hem of her dress and started to hike it up. "I wasn't planning to see you today. You told me you were busy. But now you're in my bedroom. I think we both know what that means."

"I... I... I..." He was distracting her with his lips on her neck and his hand on her bottom. "I didn't know you would be half-naked when I came here."

"But you came here." His lips went to her throat, and he proceeded to give her slow, hot openmouthed kisses. "You wanted to see me." He hooked his thumb into her underwear and, in one of the slickest moves she had ever seen, pulled them down single-handedly. She couldn't stop him even if she had wanted to. He made her insides liquid. He turned her knees to jelly. She found herself landing on his bed.

"I can't stop thinking about you," Derek whispered into her ear as his body settled on top of hers. "I hate you for it. I've never wanted anyone as much as I want you."

"I'm not sure I'm ready for this, but I want you too much to stop."

He froze and shifted their bodies so that they were on their sides and face-to-face. "I'll wait for you. I told you I would, and I meant it. I'll wait until you're ready."

This was one of those times she didn't want Derek to be such a gentleman. She wasn't sure she was ever going to be ready. She was afraid she was going to need one big push to make her finally move on for good. Even though Max had betrayed her, they had had some great times. It was true that he didn't stir any of the feelings inside her that Derek did, but there had to be something about him that made her want to spend the rest of her life with him. And if she was willing to do that, it must have been something big, right? Big enough to make her ignore all those little signs that kept popping up. Maybe she was making the same mistakes with Derek. Maybe she was ignoring all the little signs that should send her running for the hills. But the big difference with Derek was that she wasn't planning to make a life with him. She wasn't even planning on staying on the island forever.

She should let herself have this fling. Let herself enjoy this beautiful man who just wanted her for her. But Derek just wasn't the type to have a fling with. At least not for her. He would end up meaning too much to her.

"I came over here for a reason, and it wasn't to have my underwear stripped off." She rolled away from him for a moment to retrieve the open package she'd brought for him. "I thought this was for me, but when I opened it I realized it was for you."

"Is Max sending me diamonds now, too?" He winced a little as he took the package from her.

"Your hand." She took it and studied it. His cut looked angry. "It needs to be cleaned again and wrapped."

"Stop looking at me like that. This is how we got here in the first place." He shut his eyes and rested his head on her chest. "Just tell me what's in the package."

"It's a very fancy invitation."

"For what? Did you decide to get married again and invite me this time?"

"No, you ass. There's a gala in Miami, honoring local politicians who have made a difference in their communities. They want to honor you. There's a letter inside. You donate your salary back to the community and they cite your numerous good works."

"That's nice." He kissed her collarbone.

"That's all you have to say?"

"Yeah. I'm not going to go."

"You have to! How often do you get honored like this?"

"I don't do what I do to have some people I've never met honor me. I don't need the salary. My furniture business has been doing very well for many years. And when my neighbors need me, I help. I don't deserve a damn thing for doing what I'm supposed to do."

"You're so good, it's sickening."

"I'm not that good. I do it for selfish reasons."

"You are good. I have no underwear on and I'm in your

# YOUR PARTICIPATION IS REQUESTED!

Dear Reader,

Since you are a lover of our books – we would like to get to know you!

Inside you will find a short Reader's Survey. Sharing your answers with us will help our editorial staff understand who you are and what activities you enjoy.

To thank you for your participation, we would like to send you 2 books and 2 gifts – **ABSOLUTELY FREE!**

Enjoy your gifts with our appreciation,

*Pam Powers*

**SEE INSIDE
FOR READER'S
SURVEY**

# For Your Reading Pleasure...

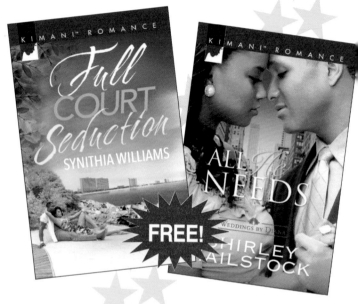

We'll send you 2 books and 2 gifts
**ABSOLUTELY FREE**
just for completing our Reader's Survey!

# YOUR READER'S SURVEY
## "THANK YOU" FREE GIFTS INCLUDE:
- ▶ 2 FREE books
- ▶ 2 lovely surprise gifts

**PLEASE FILL IN THE CIRCLES COMPLETELY TO RESPOND**

**1)** What type of fiction books do you enjoy reading? (Check all that apply)
- ○ Suspense/Thrillers  ○ Action/Adventure  ○ Modern-day Romances
- ○ Historical Romance  ○ Humor  ○ Paranormal Romance

**2)** What attracted you most to the last fiction book you purchased on impulse?
- ○ The Title  ○ The Cover  ○ The Author  ○ The Story

**3)** What is usually the greatest influencer when you <u>plan</u> to buy a book?
- ○ Advertising  ○ Referral  ○ Book Review

**4)** How often do you access the internet?
- ○ Daily  ○ Weekly  ○ Monthly  ○ Rarely or never

**5)** How many NEW paperback fiction novels have you purchased in the past 3 months?
- ○ 0 - 2  ○ 3 - 6  ○ 7 or more

**YES!** I have completed the Reader's Survey. Please send me the 2 FREE books and 2 FREE gifts (gifts are worth about $10 retail) for which I qualify. I understand that I am under no obligation to purchase any books, as explained on the back of this card.

### 168/368 XDL GLN7

| | |
|---|---|
| FIRST NAME | LAST NAME |

ADDRESS

APT.#    CITY

STATE/PROV.    ZIP/POSTAL CODE

K-217-SUR17

bed and you stopped yourself from making love to me, even when I told you I would, that I wanted to."

"I can still make you feel good. I just need to use my other hand. Switch sides with me."

"No."

"You want me to use my mouth instead?" He sat up. "I can do that."

She grabbed his arm and pulled him back down. "I didn't mean that, but I do like that. You are seriously good at that. I meant that I could do something just for you." She rolled him onto his back and kissed his chest. "Maybe I can use my mouth and hands and do some other creative things that will blow your mind."

"Blow my mind? Somebody is feeling a little cocky."

She looked down at the erection tenting his underwear. "I'm not feeling a little cocky, but you're looking a lot cocky."

He threw his head back and laughed as he grabbed her and wrapped his arms around her. "This is why I can't get enough of you."

"Kiss me again."

"I won't be able to stop." He kissed along her jaw.

"Good, because I think I might have changed my mind."

"No think. No might. Be sure. I'm sure."

She might fall for him. Really fall for him. She didn't want to, but if she let this go further, she knew she wouldn't be able to stop it.

It was going to go further, because his mouth was pressed to his and his hand was on her cheek and their bodies were lined up just right.

"Ava." She heard her name called and broke her kiss with Derek.

"I don't want to stop yet."

"Did you hear that?"

"No. I was too focused on the woman beneath me."

"Ava." She hadn't imagined it. Her name was being called from outside the house, and she recognized the voice.

"Shit. It's my big brother. Get off me!" She shoved Derek off her and yanked down her dress, not sure where her underwear had gone.

"Relax. You're an adult. He can't punish you."

"He already thinks I make poor life choices. He's not going to be thrilled that I'm in bed with a man so soon after my wedding was canceled."

"You think I'm some kind of dumb mistake."

"I just think you're dumb. Not a mistake."

"You're really taking a shot at me right now?"

"Yes." She kissed his mouth and ran down the stairs and out of her house just as Carlos was making his way across the lawn to Derek's.

"Elias, she's over here."

"Elias is here?"

"Yeah, why the hell were you in Derek's house?"

"Because he's my neighbor and I was dropping off a package?"

"Were you dropping one off or receiving one?"

"Carlos! I can't believe you just said that."

"Your lips are swollen. Your dress is rumpled, and you look like you've been rolling around on the floor. Oh, and you're not wearing any shoes. Plus, I heard you have been seen in town with him a few times."

"He's my neighbor! And I haven't slept with him. But even if I did, it would be none of your damn business because I'm single and he's single and—"

"Is he good to you?"

That question made her pause. "What?"

"Is he good to you?"

Ava sighed. "Yes. Very much so."

"It's fine with me."

"What?"

"Get your ears checked, Ava. I said whatever you two are up to is fine with me. You know I hated Max and I don't think you should spend any more time hung up on him."

"I don't think so, either."

"Where the hell were you?" Her twin emerged from her house and met them in the driveway.

"I was with Derek. Do you have your doctor bag with you?"

"I have a first-aid kit. Carlos picked me up from the ferry. It's in the car. Why?"

Derek's front door open, and he came out of his house, thankfully fully clothed. But Ava would be lying if she said she didn't miss the sight of his beautiful body. "This is why." She went over to Derek, grabbed his good hand and pulled him over to Elias. "Look. I've been trying to get him to go to the hospital."

She extended Derek's hand to show Elias.

"Damn, Ava!" Carlos frowned at her. "What were you two up to?"

"There's nothing going on, you ass face! He hurt his hand working."

"It's nice to see that I'm not the only one she verbally abuses," Derek said, grinning at her. "But she's right. I cut it making a chair."

"This is a nasty cut," Elias said. "We need to flush it to make sure there are no particulates inside."

"Do you think he needs stitches?" Ava asked, seeing that his wound was still angry-looking. She felt guilty that she had gotten him all worked up instead of seeing to his hand first.

"I have liquid stitches in my bag. I think you'll be fine with that, but you might want to go to the hospital anyway and see what they say."

"No. You sew people up for a living. I trust you."

Elias nodded. "Come inside. Carlos, can you grab my

bag out of your car? Ava, go inside, grab your bottle of per-
oxide and meet me in your kitchen."

Elias had spoken with such authority that everyone
moved without question, and before Ava could realize what
was happening, her brothers were bonding with Derek.

## Chapter 11

Derek stood on the beach down the road from his house with his cousin Hallie. Somehow this day had turned into a party. In a small town it was hard to find families that were not connected, and his family and Ava's were no different. Hallie was married to Carlos's brother-in-law. The two men worked together, and when Elias suggested they fire up the grill, it was Carlos who picked up the phone and invited him over.

"So…" Hallie said with a grin.

"So…" Derek said back to her.

"You want to tell me what's going on?"

"Not much. I got the list of vendors for the founder's day celebration this morning. We're still looking for a band to play the night of the dance. I'd hate to go off-island, but I think we might have to."

"Don't do that." She folded her arms across her chest.

"Don't do what?"

"Mayor me. You know exactly what I'm talking about."

He did. "I don't."

"Don't play coy. You can't even hide it. It's one thing to be seen all over town with her when you have never even been seen on a date with anyone. But it's the way you look at her, Derek. My God." She touched her heart. "It makes me want to cry."

"Stop being so dramatic, Hallie."

"She makes you smile."

"She's funny," he countered.

"She makes you happy."

"We're friends."

"You're in love with her."

He paused briefly at her words. *Love? No.* He had never been in love. He wasn't planning on falling in love, and if he was, he wouldn't fall for someone like Ava. "Now you're being ridiculous. I like her. That's not a secret. She's gorgeous and sweet and smart. It's hard not to like her." As soon as he finished saying that last sentence he realized how it directly contradicted his thoughts.

Why wouldn't he want to fall in love with a beautiful, sweet woman?

Ava and Elias walked up to them before Hallie could say any more. The twins were both wearing their bathing suits. Ava was wearing that same pinup-girl two-piece that he had once peeled off her. He remembered every detail of that night. He dreamed about it. And then there was this morning. Her underwear was still on the floor in his bedroom and every time he looked at her today, he knew that her bottom was bare beneath her dress. He had to physically stop himself from running his hand over her behind just to feel what he knew wasn't there.

"I love your bathing suit, Ava," Hallie said. "It's adorable."

"I like it, too," he said to her when she got closer. He felt a punch to his arm that sent pain all the way up his shoulder.

He looked over to Elias, who was stoned-faced. "Stop looking at my sister like that. This is the third time I caught you staring."

"Don't hit him!" Ava gave her twin a shove and wrapped a protective arm around Derek. "He's already injured, you jackass. And it's none of your concern how he looks at me. Maybe I like it."

"Yeah, but the rest of us don't need to know what you two like, and we certainly don't need to see what he's thinking."

"You've become a stuffy prude lately."

"A stuffy prude?"

"Yes, Doctor. Humorless, not as fun." Ava frowned at her brother. "Heal thyself."

"I'm humorless? Everyone thought you were an ice princess when you were with that last guy, and now you have the nerve to say that I'm humorless."

"Yup." She stuck her tongue out at him.

Elias shook his head. "Come on, Hallie. Let's go see what the adults are up to."

"I'd rather see you fight with your sister. My husband is a twin. I enjoy watching him and his sister argue, too."

"Twin sisters." He shook his head again. "Always starting something."

Hallie laughed, and they both walked out, leaving Derek and Ava alone for the first time since they were in his bedroom that morning. Ava was pressed against him, one of her arms loosely wrapped around him. He loved the way she felt around him and next to him and beneath him.

"You didn't have to defend me just now."

"Nobody gets to pick on you but me." She picked up his bandaged hand and kissed it. "I like picking on you. It brings me joy."

"You know they all think we're a couple now."

"It's because of the way you look at me. Damn it, Derek. I felt like my skin was on fire."

"I can't help it. Everything you do turns me on."

"I want to tell you to stop it. It's damned inconvenient to be this turned on all day, but I can't."

"Why?"

"Because no one has ever looked at me the way you do, and it makes me feel good."

"I can't help it. You are the most beautiful woman in the entire state of Florida."

"Sometimes the only thing I think I have to offer anyone is a pretty face. It was the only reason Max wanted me."

"That's not true."

"It is." She titled her head and studied him for a long moment. "It's really bugging me that you aren't going to that gala. You're getting into heaven already. You don't have to be that humble."

"I'm not being humble. I didn't tell you the entire truth before because I was too focused on getting you naked. That isn't the first time I've received that invitation. I've known about it for a while. I don't want to go, because I don't want to run into my father. I know he has been involved with the organization that's throwing the event for years."

"Now I really think you should go to show him how amazing you are."

He pressed his lips to hers, not caring who saw them or what they thought. "You think I'm amazing?"

"Of course *I* don't, but other people seem to think so. You can get dressed up in a gorgeous tux and walk into the room, looking confident and sexy."

"You think I'm sexy?" He grinned at her and bent his head to kiss her again. It was longer than the last kiss, and she shut her eyes and went pliant.

"Stop trying to distract me," she said when he broke the kiss. "I'm trying to talk to you."

"Ava, I don't own a tux. I don't even know where to get one. I don't need to prove anything to my father."

"How many people who look like you or me get honored for their brains, for the good work that they do instead of shooting a basket or hitting a ball? My brother is a baseball legend. Drafted right out of high school. Do you know his biggest regret is not going to college? He's been taking online classes."

"I didn't know that, but that's great. I'm happy he wants to pursue an education, but I'm not sure what that has to do with me."

"Nothing was handed to you when everything could have been. You could have been an entitled, egotistical jerk, but you worked your way through school. And for this town for free. You're always kind, and you give away your time and expect nothing in return and I'm proud of you. It might be meaningless but I want you to get a stupid plaque and I want you to hang it on the wall and I want that little symbol to be a sign of all the things that you do for everyone else. You don't do anything selfish! You don't do a single thing just for yourself, and for once I want you to stop being such a damn saint and get the applause and take it all in. Be indulgent."

She stomped away from him then, leaving him somewhat bewildered. Ava was wrong. He was selfish and indulgent, and he often did just think about himself. Every moment he spent with her was proof of that. He always kept his affairs private, he never spoke about the women he had been seeing and he sure as hell never brought them to the island. He didn't want talk of his love life to overshadow his work on the island, but with Ava he didn't give a crap about any of that. He didn't care that she had just gotten out of a long-term relationship. He didn't care whether or not it was the right time or if she might still have some lingering feelings for her ex. He just wanted to be with her, hear her voice, smell her scent and have her near.

And for the first time in his life, he didn't give a damn about what anyone thought about it.

A few days later Derek drove to his mother's house. On his way to fix the thing she had called him about a couple of weeks ago. It wasn't like him to put things off. But he had been on such a high lately with Ava that dealing with his mother would bring him down, and he didn't want to feel that way. Still he knew he couldn't avoid her forever.

She was home. Her car was the only one in the driveway, and he heard the faint sounds from the television. He knocked on the door, feeling awkward every time he was there, like this wasn't his childhood home. There was no welcoming feeling, no familiarity, no warmth spreading through him as he waited to be let in.

The door opened, and his mother stood there in a slinky dress and bare feet. Her face was made up. She was a beautiful woman, and he knew it was sexist and small-minded of him to wish she covered up, but he did. She had been dressing like this his entire life. Whenever she did show up to school functions, it was always in sky-high heels and tight dresses and other clothes that looked like they were meant more for Miami nightlife than small-town island living.

He had to endure endless jokes about how sexy his mother was from his classmates. His first fistfight was about her. His last fight was, too. But it was with one of her boyfriends, who got a little too rough with her one night.

"Hello, sweetheart." She was surprised to see him. "I'm happy to see you."

He nodded his head. "I got your message. I thought I would stop by and fix the bathroom door. You're alone?"

"Yes. I was just starting dinner. Would you like to stay?"

He nodded. "Just show me what needs to be fixed and I'll get on it."

It didn't take him long to fix the few things that needed tending to in the house. It was more work than she had originally asked him to do. She kept finding things that needed his attention. He was fine with that because the more he worked, the less awkward conversation they would have to make.

He finished up and headed to the kitchen to see her plating the meal she had just cooked. "Sit down, Derek." She motioned to the table. "I'll serve you. It will be like old times."

He could count on one hand the times she had served him dinner. Special occasions, like when she felt incredibly guilty about something. The last time had been when she missed his first swearing-in ceremony. He took a seat at the small table and noticed a pair of designer men's sunglasses there.

"Are you still seeing that guy you introduced me to at Hack's?"

"Yes!" She beamed and got a dreamy look in her eye. She almost looked like a teenage girl. "He's a wonderful man. He treats me like a princess. I've never felt this way about anyone. He could be the one."

He had heard that before. More times than he could count. It always ended in heartbreak. "That's nice, Mom. I'm happy for you."

"What's going on with you? Anything new?"

"We're finalizing the details for the founder's day celebrations. You should bring your friend to the dance."

"I will. He gets a kick out of that cutesy little stuff." She set a plate down in front of him.

"The entire town is involved. All the proceeds go to charity. I don't think it's so cutesy or little." She always did that, put this island and everything that went on in it down. She had been dying to get out of here her entire life, but when things fell apart, it was the only place she could return to that always welcomed her back with open arms.

"I didn't mean it like that. I'm sure it's going to be very nice. I know you work very hard on it every year."

He nodded, not wanting to argue with her. They never argued. Maybe that was the problem. He just swallowed stuff until it became a rock-hard ball of anger in his stomach. He could never come out and tell her how he really felt. "I'm being honored. The Business in Action Coalition is giving me an award. There's going to be a gala in Miami in a few weeks."

Her head snapped up at that. "Is your father going to be there?"

"I don't know."

"I know he's been in that group for some time. Have you spoken to him?"

"I haven't spoken to him in years."

"He'll probably be there. Do you think he'll bring his wife? She has to know who you are. All of Miami does."

"The organization is huge. Victor isn't even at the head of it. They have a lot of events. I'm not even sure he knows I'm being honored."

"Your father knows everything that goes on in Miami." She took an agitated bite of her dinner. "Do you need a date? I would be happy to go with you." Just so she could see him. She didn't give a damn about what Derek did to get honored. She was so hung up on Victor, on the man who didn't love her enough, on the man who told her over and over that she would never be good enough. How could she still be in love with him?

"I don't think I'm going to go."

"Oh?" She seemed disappointed, but not for the same reasons that Ava was disappointed. "Why aren't you eating? Is there something wrong with the food?"

He looked down at his plate of salmon and some sort of zucchini side dish. "No. I've been feeling under the weather for the past few days."

"Maybe salmon isn't the best thing for you."

"No." He stood up. "I think I'm going to head home. I've got a busy day tomorrow."

She stood up, too, and lightly kissed his cheek. "See you around, honey."

"Yeah." Probably the next time she needed something.

## Chapter 12

There was a storm coming. Not a huge one, but one big enough to set Ava on edge. The island felt a little different. The air was thicker, the trees swayed a little harder and there was that ominous roll of thunder in the distance. She should be used to thunderstorms by now. She had lived in Florida for many years, but as many storms as she had been through, she never felt at ease during one. It was something she should have grown out of, but she never did.

She went to her living room to look up at the quickly darkening sky and she saw Derek's truck pull into the driveway. She hadn't seen him in days. Three to be exact. She had yelled at him the last time they were together. She was embarrassed about it. She never allowed herself to yell. She was always yelling at him, or arguing with him, but that day she got really upset with him, too upset with him for something that shouldn't matter so much to her. She realized that she cared about him and it was more than just surface concern. It went so much deeper. She wanted more for him than he wanted for himself, and she wasn't sure how that had happened, or why it was happening so fast.

It scared her, and she wanted to stay away from him. For real this time, but being away from him didn't mean that she didn't think about him. She had seen his grandmother. Gone shopping with his aunts, even gone back to the senior center to have tea with some women there and he had come up in every conversation. No one asked about them, which she always thought was coming; they just talked about the good things Derek was doing for the community that didn't seem like such a big deal to him at all.

He looked up at her, and their eyes connected. Without her saying a word or making a motion he started to walk toward her house. She had wanted him to come over. She had gotten used to sharing her meals with him, and when he wasn't there, eating seemed like a lonely thing.

She opened the door as another rumble of thunder rolled through the air. She stiffened slightly, knowing the storm was going to be a big one.

"You're wearing real shoes," he said by way of greeting.

"And a dress with a zipper." She turned around to show him. "I've even put on makeup. I do believe I'm making progress. By the end of the month, I will have morphed back into a lady."

"You don't need any of those things to be a lady. You're naturally one."

"Don't be sweet to me. I thought we talked about that." A purple streak of lightning raced through the sky and sent the hairs on the back of her neck standing. "Come inside." She grabbed his hand.

"The storm is making you nervous."

She nodded, admitting to him what she had never admitted to anyone. Elias knew, but for everyone else she pretended to be unbothered.

"It won't be so bad. Hurricane season probably won't be the best time to be here."

"I'll probably be gone by then," she said, feeling a little twinge. She knew she couldn't stay here forever. She had a life to get on with. A life without Derek, without this island.

"Yeah," he said slowly. "It might be for the best."

She still had his hand. His warm, calloused fingers felt comforting to her for some reason.

"I have ingredients. Tonight, I will cook for us." She gave him a small smile, feeling awkward with him.

"Cook. You know how to do that? I was sure you snapped your fingers and some servant did that for you."

"Only when I was with Max. I have cooked before."

"You're not going to make anything with kale, are you? Because that is my worst nightmare."

"Nope, no kale. How do you feel about a brussels sprout, beet and broccoli salad? I can whip that up in a few minutes."

He just stared at her. She tried to suppress a grin, but she couldn't help it.

"Gotcha." She pulled him into the kitchen and sat him down at the small table while she looked in the refrigerator. "I've got chicken breast and a pork tenderloin and salmon." She stood there and looked at him. "No salmon tonight. You don't like it. I could make pasta. Creamy, garlicky pasta with chicken. I can add spinach to it. Do you like spinach?"

Without getting up from his chair, Derek grabbed her arm and tugged her into his lap. And then he kissed her. It was hard to describe the reaction her body had whenever Derek's lips touched hers. Usually she felt like her skin was on fire and the only way to cool off was to take off all her clothes and press her body to his, but this time she felt more in his kiss. It was deeper and sweeter and in that kiss she could feel…him. His feelings. She could sense that something was up when she opened the door, but she knew for sure right then.

"Okay." She moved herself from his lap. "Pasta it is."

"How did you know I didn't like salmon?"

"You told me. You said it was the only fish you didn't like."

"You remembered?"

"Yes, Derek." She nodded. "I value you for more than just your sexy body. I listen when you talk."

He grabbed her hand and pulled her close, resting his head against her stomach as he wrapped his arms around her hips. "Come with me to the gala."

"You're going?" She stroked his head.

"Yes."

"Because I yelled at you or because I remembered you don't like salmon?"

"Both. No one yells at me. I like it."

"What about the salmon thing?"

"My mother doesn't remember that I hate it. That she made it for me and I got so violently ill that I had to go to the hospital."

"You just came from your mother's house. That's why you're in a funky mood. I thought I felt it when I saw you, but now I know."

"You know me." He looked up at her. "Better than she does, and that should be impossible, but it isn't."

"I don't know if I know you better than anyone else. I just want you to be happy, Derek. Everyone in this town wants that for you."

"What I have with you is different from what I have with everyone else, and you know it."

"That's because I let you stick your hand up my dress."

He gave her a quick grin. "Are you going to come with me to the gala?"

"You sure you want me there? What about your grandmother or your cousin? I met your aunts. They are really lovely."

"I need you there," he said as he looked into her eyes. "Just you. I won't be able to get through the night without you."

She should say no. She shouldn't even allow the closeness they were sharing at the moment, but she couldn't deny him. She wanted to be with him that night. She wanted him to be happy, and a big part of her wanted to be the one to make him happy. "We have to get you a tux. I'll need a dress to wear. I'm doubting any of my other gowns will fit me. We'll have to leave for Miami a little earlier."

"And stay a little later." He slipped his hand beneath her hem and stroked the back of her thigh. She knew what his silent message was. Miami was where they would make love. They had danced around the issue long enough. He wanted her as much as she wanted him, and after the gala she would give him her body.

Ava had definitely been uneasy on the ferry ride back to Miami. Derek had a hard time taking his eyes off her during the ride. She had nearly changed back to the woman he had met. Her makeup was done to perfection. Her dress was fitted and structured. She wore stiletto heels, but she hadn't tamed her hair. No straightener had touched it. She left it in those loose, flowing waves that he liked so much. She was a little more rigid than he was used to, than he liked, but when she looked at him there was softness in her eyes and she leaned against him slightly as they sat. He had no idea what was going on in her mind, but he was very aware that this was the first time she had been back here since she had left to get married. This was her town, with her fancy friends. This was where she rubbed shoulders with the wealthy and was a part of the fashion scene. Two things Derek knew nothing about.

He wondered if he was good enough to be seen with her. Yes, he was the mayor of a town. Yes, he was educated and a successful business owner. But he was a working-class guy. Maybe not on paper, but he felt like he was. He would never be comfortable in a suit. Never feel at home sitting behind a desk, or driving a car that was worth more than some families made in five years. And that's what Ava had been used to. Hideaway Island was a break from that all, but now that she was back here she would see that he was just a small-town guy and her life would never be a fit for him.

"This trip is always so beautiful to me. I've made it countless times, but it never stops being lovely."

"I know what you mean."

"I always feel the same way each time I make it. So excited and full of joy to be going to Hideaway Island and so sad and filled with anxiety to leave it."

Derek just looked at her, unsure how to respond to that. It wasn't what he had expected to hear.

"You look nice today." She touched his collar and then smoothed her hand over his shoulder.

"It's just non-paint-smeared jeans and a rarely worn polo. Nanny might say I look less like a homeless person."

"I like you in paint-smeared clothes, too." She gave him a shy smile as she fiddled with his collar again. "In the fashion world we would call this color ondine blue. It was the color of the summer a few years back."

"That's probably when I got this shirt."

"It does things to your eyes. Have I ever told you how beautiful your eyes are?"

"What's the matter, baby?" He wrapped his arm around her and pulled her close to him. She only got this sweet when something was up. "I can't take all these compliments. You know your salty mouth keeps my blood pumping."

She let out a little laugh. "I'm nervous."

"About me?"

"Why would I be nervous about you, dummy? I'm just not sure I'm ready to be back here. It feels like vacation is over."

"The good news is that you get to go back to Hideaway Island. In fact, if you want to, we can turn right back around as soon as we dock."

"No! This night is important for you. We're going. It's just that—that… I thought I would have my life all figured out when I came back."

"Who said you had to have your life all figured out? Why can't you just take all the time you need?"

"I don't have a job, Derek. I feel useless. I feel like I should be doing more. I spent the last few years of my life being some man's accessory."

"And you feel like tonight you're going to be mine?"

Her head snapped up. "No. I never feel that way with you. Should I? You've seen me at my worst. You don't give a damn if I'm beautiful, but I'm not sure what it is you like about me."

There were so many reasons that he liked her, the first was that she let him see a side of her that no one else got to see. There were few people in his life that he could just talk to, and she was one of them. "I saw you destroy your wedding dress with your bare hands. I'm afraid of what will happen to me if I don't like you."

She grinned at him and rested her head on his shoulder. As they got closer to land, a little uneasiness crept up inside him. He knew that this weekend would forever change things between them and he might not come back to Hideaway Island the same man as he left.

To say that the hotel Derek had booked for them was posh was an understatement. They were directly on the water with views of the Atlantic and Biscayne Bay. As soon as they walked through the doors, Ava felt like she had been transported back to when she was with Max and they only stayed in the finest places and dined on the fanciest food. She didn't expect it from Derek, though. She actually didn't know what to expect from him on this trip. The people here were so different from the ones on Hideaway Island. She had been gone for two months after spending nearly ten years in this glitzy city and yet this place felt foreign to her. No middle-class people stayed in a hotel like this. Jet-setters and high rollers and people with black cards stayed here. Last year she wouldn't have thought much about staying in a place like this, but today she looked around at high-end fixtures and wondered if any of it was worth the cost.

"What made you decide to pick this hotel, Derek?" she asked him as they entered the glass elevators.

"It's next door to the hotel where they are having the event. The other hotel was full. Some sort of convention is there."

"Oh. That makes sense." She didn't notice which floor Derek had pushed when they had walked in, but they bypassed all the lower floors in the huge hotel and the farther they went up, the more of the beautiful Miami skyline she could see.

The elevator finally came to a stop, and they walked out onto a floor with only two rooms. Ava wasn't sure why she was having trouble breathing, but she was. He opened the door to their suite, and she was greeted by a wall of glass. Unobstructed views of the ocean filled her eyes and for a moment she was at a loss for words. It wasn't just a room. There was a full living room and dining room and a long hallway that led to presumably more. On the walls there was expensive art, not the generic paintings you found at most hotels but one-of-a-kind pieces that probably cost more than her car.

"Is it okay?" he asked from behind her.

She turned around to face him. "What kind of question is that? There had to be other rooms. Why did you book this one?"

"I wanted a two-bedroom suite. This is what they had."

"We could have gotten a two-bedroom suite at a chain hotel a few blocks from here!"

"I asked you to come here with me. I wanted to take you someplace beautiful, someplace you would be comfortable staying."

"This is too much. You must really not think much of me."

"Excuse me?"

"I don't need any of this. I'm not the princess everyone thinks I am. I thought you knew me better. I could spend the night with you in a one-room shack and be happy."

"Of course we don't need any of this. No one does. But you told me to do something selfish, something just for me, and this is it. Tonight I want to give you the best for no other reason than because I can. I've worked hard my entire life. I have saved every penny I've ever earned. I've given back to my community at every opportunity. I don't do anything for myself. But being with you is the thing I do just for me. I don't care what anyone thinks or says about it. I don't care if it's not smart or if it can't work or if it's not going to last. I have been reasonable my entire life, but I can't be reasonable when it comes to you. I don't want to be reasonable when it comes to you."

All the air left Ava in that moment. If her feet weren't firmly planted on the ground, she thought she might have floated away. No one ever spoke to her like Derek did. No one had ever looked at her the way he did, or touched her, or kissed her like every time was going to be the last time.

She had been nervous coming back to Miami, nervous that she would get a glimpse of her old life and start to miss it, but she had been more nervous about being here alone with Derek. She knew she was going to fall in love with him. It was just a matter of time now. She could already feel the stirrings of it deep in her chest. She knew that she needed to prevent it from happening. To remove herself from him. To break all contact. But she didn't want to.

It could never last. Hideaway Island was a vacation for her. But she was going to let herself feel whatever she was feeling. She hadn't done that with Max. She fooled herself into thinking she was in love. She forced it because she thought marrying him was the safe choice. She thought she would always be taken care of with him and because of that she ignored every uncertainty and emotion that she had had.

She refused to do that anymore.

"Are you crying?" He took a step forward, his arms out-stretched, but she stepped back. She knew if she let him touch her, she wouldn't be able to let him go.

"Shut up. No." She swiped the tears off her face. "We don't have time for me to strip you naked and climb on top of you. We've got to go shopping."

"Screw shopping." He grabbed her hand. "I don't care if we don't leave this room for the next two weeks."

It was tempting. Especially since he was looking at her like she was a juicy steak and he had just come off a fast. "No. We have an appointment."

"One kiss."

He stepped forward and pressed his mouth to hers before she could respond. It was a hell of a kiss, filled with all the pent-up emotion and passion that had been surging inside them for weeks.

"One hour," he whispered into her lips.

"No more," she groaned and pulled herself away from him.

One hour wouldn't be enough.

She was starting to think one lifetime wouldn't even cover it.

# Chapter 13

"Navy blue?" Derek asked Ava, unsure of the tux she had put him in.

"Navy blue." She nodded. If he had to go shopping, Ava was the best person on the planet to go with. She had called in his measurements the day before they arrived, and the swanky men's boutique they were in had magically produced three tuxedos that fit him perfectly. "Navy blue, with satin lapels and a straight tie. There will be dozens of men in traditional boring black tuxedos, but you will be the young, hip mayor in navy."

"And the fit." He glanced at himself in the mirror, noticing that he could see the outline of his bicep. "You don't think it should be looser?"

"Are you insane? This tux is supposed to be fitted. Are you uncomfortable? Like you're going to burst out of it if you move the wrong way?"

"No. It's just... I can feel it."

"That's because the only thing you are used to is wearing jeans and T-shirts." She smoothed her hands across his shoulders and down his arms. "You have an amazing body that needs to be shown off. You're built like an athlete. Cartwell's knows how to properly attire men like you. Carlos gets his suits from here."

"He told you about this place?"

"Really, Derek? Your words are like a knife in my chest."

He grinned at her dramatic statement. She seemed happier than he had seen her in days just from being in this store. He had even caught her helping another man pick out dress shirts. It was clear she was in her element and that she took great pride in making people look their best. She didn't think it was important and maybe being in fashion didn't compare with what Elias did as a surgeon. But her passion was important, too, because she knew how to make people feel good about themselves. "If it doesn't have an elastic waist, my big brother doesn't wear it. I was the one who told him about this place."

"And half of his baseball team," a man said, appearing from the back of the store. "If there's one thing professional athletes know how to do, it's spend money. And Ava got the Hammerheads to spend a beachfront house's worth commission in here in the last few years. How are you, princess?" The man approached and kissed both of Ava's cheeks. "You look stunning."

"Thank you," Ava smiled prettily at him. "Derek." She turned back to him. "I want you to meet my old friend Teddy. Teddy is the fashion director for this chain of boutiques. Teddy this is my…" There was just a slight pause, just long enough for all of them to know that she was caught up on what to call him. "This is my friend Derek."

It bothered him a bit to hear her call him her friend. They were more than just friends. Way more. But in reality it was the truth. They weren't dating or committed.

They just spent a lot of time together, and he felt closer to her than he did anyone else.

"Hello, Derek," Teddy said to him. "I see Ava has chosen well for you. Perfect, color, cut and fit. Understated and yet fashion forward."

"Ava knows me better than I know myself sometimes."

"I could say the same thing about you." There was a little smile hovering on her lips, and he had the urge to kiss the smile from her mouth. This day was going to be miserably long, because it was going to be hours until they were alone. Just him and her and nothing to interrupt them. He was going to make love to her tonight. He had never waited this long for a woman. No woman had been worth waiting for before. He was counting down the minutes until he could get what he wanted.

"I was going to tell you that I was sorry about your engagement, but I see you have moved on to bigger and better things. Got yourself a politician and a clean one, too. That's like catching a unicorn."

"See, Derek." She flashed him a quick smile. "You're rare and majestic."

"Who are you working for now?" Teddy asked her. "I haven't heard you were back on the Miami scene. Are you moving up to bigger stores in New York? I always thought you should buy for Bloomies."

"I'm not back to buying yet. I have just been trying to figure out what I should be doing with my life. I've had offers in New York and even one in Tokyo before. I'm just not sure what's best for me."

"Buy for us!" Teddy took her hands. "We have to wait till Bernardo officially retires in a few months, but if you want the job, it's yours. You can set your hours. The pay is fantastic, and you'll get to travel the world to scope out the trends."

"I have never bought men's clothing before. Are you sure everyone would be on board with this?"

"Yes," he said with an emphatic shake of his head. "You have a great reputation with designers. The sales reps fall at your feet. And before you decided to quit to marry that billionaire, you were getting a job offer a week. You're perfect for this job. We're expanding all over the East Coast. We need someone like you to get us to the next level."

"That sounds amazing," she said a little breathlessly.

Derek watched Ava closely, trying to gauge how she really felt about the job offer. It was a big deal. It could propel her career. She had been wondering what she was going to do with her life, and this opportunity seemed to have fallen in her lap. He should be happy for her, but his first reaction was that he didn't want her to go.

He had no right to feel that way. He shouldn't be looking at this weekend as the start of something new. She was just out of a relationship, and he didn't want to be in one… or at least he hadn't wanted to be in one until she walked into his life.

Later that night Ava checked her appearance in the mirror for the fiftieth time. She had gone to countless events with Max where her only job was to look good, but tonight she was more worried than she had been on the arm of a billionaire. Derek was being honored simply because he was a good man. It wasn't just his small island who knew how special he was. The news had spread. There was an article about him in Miami's biggest paper, featuring a large picture of him wearing his uniform of a T-shirt and jeans, swinging a hammer as he helped rebuild a family's house that had burned down. The reporter wrote about his furniture business and his close relationship with his uncle and how he strived to do the right thing every time, even when it was hard. Ava had always known that he was a good man, and now the people outside of the little island paradise were going to know it, too. There was speculation of a Senate run. She never heard from Derek that he had political aspirations outside Hideaway Island, but if he did, he could do a lot of good for a lot of people.

Tonight he was stepping out into the world, and she was going to be with him, on his arm. People were going to judge him by her and the way she carried herself.

He should have some sweet schoolteacher on his arm. Or a powerful woman who could talk business and politics and be on top of every important matter. She was an unemployed ex-fiancée of a rich man.

There was a knock on her door, and she opened it to find Derek dressed in his tux and looking devastatingly handsome. Sometimes her heart hurt just looking at him.

"Whoa." Derek took a step back. "I—I…you're just incredible."

"Is it okay, really?" She self-consciously smoothed her hand down her side.

"Wow."

She had chosen a pale pink beaded hourglass gown. It was a vintage piece made in the 1950s. It was a garment she had been salivating over for the past few years but knew that she couldn't wear it to an event with Maxime. The dress would make her stand out. Max just wanted her to be the pretty, well-spoken ornament on his arm. But with Derek she felt safe enough to wear it. He didn't care about what she put on her body because she was more than just a pretty face to him.

"I don't have enough words, Ava. I don't think there is one perfect enough to describe how amazing you look tonight."

He was handsome, too, almost devastatingly so. Yet she still preferred him in jeans and a T-shirt with paint on his clothes and the faint scent of wood on his skin.

She leaned forward, placing her hands on his chest, and kissed him softly. "I'm nervous," she admitted.

"Why should you be nervous? Those people are going to take one look at me and wonder how the hell I ended up with someone like you."

"I'm afraid of the same thing."

He looked at her for a long moment. His face unreadable, he just reached out and took her hand, locking his fingers with hers. "I didn't go my prom."

"No?"

"My mother…" He shook his head. "Long story. I've never done this. Gotten dressed up and showed up at a girl's door to take her somewhere fancy. You've done this a million times."

"I went to four proms. I was even queen at my own."

"Show-off."

She nodded and grinned at him. "I was kind of a big deal in school."

"All this time I was thinking you were a princess when you really were a queen. I got you something." He pulled her out of her room and into the living room. The sun was just setting, and all she could see out of their wall of windows was orange sky and calm ocean.

"Thank you," she said to him.

"I didn't give you anything yet. You might not even like it."

"Thank you for bringing me here. Thank you for this day."

"I didn't do anything. I just rented a hotel room." He picked up a small white box off the end table. "I didn't want to get you jewelry because I know you got enough of it these past couple of months to open a jewelry store. I thought about getting you a puppy or a kitten, but it might be a pain getting it on the ferry—plus we have a shelter full of adoptable cats and dogs back on the island."

"You're such a mayor." She laughed.

"Just open the box." He handed it to her.

It was a corsage. It was a simple ivory rose attached to a pearl bracelet. It was understated and beautiful. "Oh…" For the second time that day she felt like crying.

"You don't have to wear it. I just wanted you to be the woman I gave my first corsage to."

She shut her eyes for a moment and held out her wrist. "Put it on me."

"Are you sure? I never meant for you to wear it. I just wanted to give it to you."

"Put it on me, dummy."

Derek slid it on to her wrist and then kissed her hand. He was grinning at her, and she knew that this moment was one of the sweetest in her life.

"Thank you for today, Ava. I appreciate you."

"You're welcome." She turned so that her back was facing him. "Now unzip my dress and take me to your bedroom."

He let out a loud bark of laughter and pulled her into a tight hug. "You've got me in a tux. I'm showing it off." He dropped his voice to a whisper and spoke into her ear. "I can't wait to get you back here tonight. I've wanted you since the moment I laid eyes on you."

"The moment you laid eyes on me? That can't be right. I was engaged to Max then."

"I know." He kissed below her ear. "Come on—let's go."

## Chapter 14

It was a short walk to the hotel next door, and as Derek and Ava made their way to the ballroom where the event was being held he couldn't help but feel that this was all surreal. He didn't think he would ever be here.

He didn't go to galas. He didn't rub elbows with the rich. It never appealed to him because that seemed to be the only thing that his mother ever wanted out of life. "This place is really incredible," Ava said to him in awe.

It was beautiful, lavish by anyone's standards. There was a red carpet leading the way to the doors, and on each side of it were live tall trees filled with blooming white flowers. She must have traveled the world with her ex, seen equally stunning places, but she always managed to find the beauty in all things, even the small things. He loved that about her.

"It is." It was like the organizers of the event had brought nature inside. There were thousands of flowers inside the ballroom. Blooms in every color imaginable and they had lined every inch of the room almost making it feel as if they were in a rain forest. It represented Miami with its tropical, colorful elegance.

They checked in and were seated at a table toward the front. He felt completely out of his element. The governor of Florida was seated at the next table. There was a congressman four chairs away from him, and some of Miami's most powerful businesspeople were there. On paper he supposed he belonged. He owned a very successful business and could command thousands of dollars for a single custom-made piece. But he wasn't in his business for the love of money. He was in it because he loved what he did. He loved to work with his hands. He loved when he turned nothing into something.

Ava slipped her hand into his and leaned against him. "You belong here."

"What?" Derek frowned at her.

"You belong here just as much as anyone else does. I wanted to remind you."

Was she in his head? Was she reading his thoughts? Or did she just know him that well.

"I was smart and brought the right date. You'll smack my hand if I pick up the wrong fork, won't you?"

"You want to know a secret?" She shut her eyes and rested her head on his shoulder. "I had no idea what I was doing at all those events with Max. But I was really good at pretending that I wasn't a total poseur."

"Damn it, Ava. If you didn't belong, then no one does."

"I grew up in a tiny three-bedroom house. My father worked in a factory. My mother worked two jobs. We lived paycheck to paycheck. I don't know anything about etiquette. The fanciest dinners we had were at chain restaurants. I looked good on Max's arm. Exotic. You think I don't know that? You think I don't know what people at these events thought of me?"

"What did they think of you? Anyone who speaks to you for more than five seconds can see how incredible you are."

"It took you a lot longer than five seconds." She grinned up at him.

"It took me a little while to get over your horrific taste in men."

"Me, too." She sighed. "I found myself thinking about my father a tremendous amount these past few months. Sometimes I think my wedding falling apart was his doing."

"Really?"

"He would have hated Max, too." She laughed. "And he wouldn't have been able to hide it."

"I would have loved your father."

"He would have loved you, too," she said quietly, with an undeniable tinge of sadness to her voice. "We're here tonight to celebrate you and so that you can make connections or do whatever you politicians do."

He pressed his forehead against hers. "I'm here because you yelled at me. I don't need to make any more connections. All my connections are on Hideaway Island. I just wanted to have a nice evening with the beautiful woman that drives me insane."

"Son?" Derek felt a tap on his other shoulder. It had been a few years, but the sound of his father's voice was unmistakable. He had tried not to think about his father this trip. He had been hoping that he had nothing to do with this honor, that Derek's work in his community spoke for itself, but he was afraid he had been wrong. That this was just some ploy by his father.

He sat up and turned to look at Victor, who seemed not to have aged at all. He was a handsome man, his hair just going gray at his temples. He wore an elegant black tux, and the way he held himself told the story of how undeniably powerful he was.

It was odd looking at him, because Derek could see so

many of his own physical features. Even if his father wanted to hide that he was his son, he couldn't. The world would know from just seeing them together.

"Hello, Mr.—"

"Don't. I'm your father and I love you. You don't go by my last name, but I refuse to be called Mr. Bernal by you."

His strong words surprised Derek. He expected some strained small talk, but his father wasn't messing around.

"Did you have something to do with getting me this award?"

"No. A committee decides. I found out when everyone else did. Very frankly I didn't think you would show up, but I'm glad you did. I've been wanting to speak to you face-to-face for years. Do you think we could talk somewhere in private for a few minutes?"

He looked back at Ava, feeling her gaze on him. "This is Ava, Dad. Ava this is my father, Victor Bernal."

"Ava Bradley?" His eyes narrowed a bit. "You were engaged to Max Vermeulen. We've met before."

"It's nice to see you again."

"You're with my son now?" There was a little bit of judgment in his father's voice that Derek wasn't sure he liked. He looked to Ava to see her reaction to the question, but she kept her face neutral and slipped her fingers between his.

"Yes." She nodded. "He's my neighbor on Hideaway Island and a friend of my family. He helped me get through a hard time."

"What the hell happened with you and Max? He's crazy about you."

"I found out that he has a longtime mistress and three children. That when he told me he's traveling for business that he was really vacationing with his other family. Call me old-fashioned, but I virtually insist upon my husband being truthful and faithful."

His father sputtered, and for the first time Derek saw

the man completely at a loss. He would have kissed Ava right then and there if he could.

"You've told her everything about us?"

"Everything." He nodded.

"Can we go somewhere and talk alone?"

He was about to say no, make it another three years till he spoke to him again, but Ava squeezed his hand. "Go on, Derek. I'll be fine here."

"Are you sure?"

She leaned forward and kissed his cheek. "Yes, but don't take too long. You know how much I love millionaires. I might end up engaged to another one by the time you come back."

He felt a little kick in his chest at her words. Hallie had accused him of being in love with her. Carlos said he was a goner. He had thought she'd been reading too much into it, but he could see himself falling in love with Ava. Forever in love and if she were anyone else that thought wouldn't scare him. But he knew that she was temporarily in his life and he learned a long time ago to stop wishing for things that could never be. His parents had taught him that lesson.

He stood up and led the way out of the room and into a semiprivate seating area. They didn't sit; instead they stood face-to-face, looking at each other. Same height, same build, same light-colored eyes. Even similar backgrounds. His father was a self-made man and so was Derek. But they were fundamentally different, because Derek could never willingly hurt someone he cared about.

"What do you want to talk about?"

"I'm sorry," Victor said instantly. "I just wanted to tell you that, and that I'm proud of you."

"What exactly are you sorry for?"

"For what I tried to do with you and your brother. I wanted to light a fire under him and let you know at the same time that I loved you and that you were part of my family even if you were not a product of my marriage. I knew I went about it the wrong way, and I'm sorry."

"Do you want my forgiveness?"

"I want you in my life, damn it."

"I have so much going on right now. It's too complicated to have a relationship with you."

"Because of your mother?"

"Yes, because of my mother. Because of the fact that she's still in love with you after all these years and can't function whenever you're in the picture."

"I still love your mother, too, but we are toxic for each other. Don't you think I wanted it to work out between us?"

"How could it have worked out? Were you going to leave your wife? Or just keep screwing around behind her back."

"I may not be the honorable man you are, but I did nothing behind my wife's back. You were never a secret from her. We have an open union. We didn't marry out of love. I was Cuban immigrant with a lot of power and a hell of a lot of money. She was a broke society girl who could elevate me in social circles that I could never dream of being in. We both had relationships outside of our marriage. The youngest girl in our family is not even my daughter. So if you're concerned for her well-being, don't be. We both get something out of our relationship, and it works."

"Because you're both lacking morally."

"Don't judge something you know nothing about." He shook his head. "I don't want to fight with you. I want to know you. I've been following your career. Both careers. I have your pieces in my office."

"I've never sent anything to you."

"You think I'm stupid enough to order under my own name?" He grinned at him. "The twelve-foot bookshelf shaped like a tree."

"That was you? That was a damn good tree."

"It was." He nodded. "And so are your leadership skills.

Your town was on the verge of bankruptcy. You boosted the economy and created programs for children and the elderly. You play fair, and everyone likes you. I could never get by in life that way."

"It's not hard, Dad. You just do what's right and stick to it."

"I'm not sure how you got to be who you are, but you are someone I admire greatly."

"Uncle Hal showed me by example. He was a great husband and father and a kind man. I wanted to be just like him," he said truthfully, not concerned about his father's feelings in that moment. He missed his uncle every day.

"I wish I could have known him. But it's not too late for me to know you."

"We can't just make up for lost time. I'm not sure what you want from me."

"Dinner. Or lunch. Hell, we can just have coffee. I want time. That's all." His father was asking for time, while his mother couldn't seem to spare any. It seemed wrong to deny him.

"Fine. Okay. Call me next week, and I promise I will pick up."

"Good. There's buzz about a Senate run for you. If you want to do it, let me know and I'll fund it."

That comment caused Derek's body to jerk. "Excuse me?"

"My company has been reporting record profits for the last five years. Funding you is a much better way of spending my money than sinking it into another boat."

"I'm not talking about the funding. I'm talking about the Senate. What are you talking about?"

"You haven't heard? There was a big write-up about you in the *Miami Record* this morning. I'm surprised no one has contacted you about it yet."

"I had no clue. I'm not sure where they got that information from. I have never expressed interest in a national politics."

"You don't have to. People are seeing all the good you're doing, and they want you to enact change on a larger level. Why do you think this organization is honoring you? This is their way of giving you their endorsement. You're young and honest and energetic, and you've won over business owners. The election is yours, Derek. All you have to do is announce."

"I... I can't think about this right now." It was too much. The idea of enacting change on a greater level sounded appealing, but he liked his life on his sleepy island. He loved his business. He would have to give that up. He just wasn't ready.

"Okay, can we talk about Ava for a moment?"

Ava...the longer he was around her the more he wanted her. It was more than just physical. It was hard to imagine what life would be like without her. He had grown accustomed to being with her every day. His day didn't feel complete until he saw her smile. He knew she was going to take that job with Cartwell's, but what he didn't know was how he was going to get through the day after she was gone.

"What about her?"

"Are you sure she's not dating you to get back at Max?"

"Of course I'm sure."

"She's stunning, Derek. But she reminds me of your mother."

"She looks nothing like Mom."

"No. But your mother was another stunning beauty who only dated wealthy men and seemed to jump into relationships quickly."

"Ava is not Mom," he said hearing the steel in his voice. He had initially thought that about her, too. He shouldn't be angry at his father for pointing it out, but he was. Ava was sweet and vulnerable and kind. She wasn't his mother.

"Your mother went out with an associate of mine soon after we broke up. She did it to make me jealous, and I was. She was pregnant with you two months later. I'm just warning you to be careful."

"Careful so I don't get trapped with a kid. Like you got trapped with me."

"Now, Derek…"

"Never mind. I left her alone in there. I need to get back to her."

Derek was slightly on edge when he returned. The outside world may have not noticed, because he was smiling, charming and everything a great politician should be. But Ava felt that he was a little tighter than before. His parents had this effect on him, and once again she was amazed how different her life had been. How lucky she was to have two parents who loved and supported her unconditionally. Derek needed that. Just to be loved for no reason at all.

There was a lull when no one was engaging him in conversation. He was standing close to the bar, a glass of scotch in his hand. She walked over to him, wrapped her arms around him and rested her face against his chest. She knew this wasn't the right place to show him this type of affection, but she couldn't make her body stop itself from connecting with his, and she couldn't help but feel that he needed to be hugged.

"You're fading out on me, Mr. Mayor."

"Am I? You want to get out of here?"

"We can't." She looked up at him. "In five minutes they are going to call your name, and you are going to go up there and say something. Then we are going to eat a flourless chocolate cake. We can leave after that."

"No dancing? There's a band."

"I'll dance with you. But later in the hotel room. You'll be naked. It will be fun."

He cupped her face in his warm hand and pressed a kiss to her lips. "You're supposed to be convincing me to stay. Not to leave here as fast as humanly possible."

"How was the talk with your father?"

"It was fine. He wants to spend some time with me. I agreed. He's easier to deal with than my mother."

"He's so handsome. You look so much like him. I wonder if you'll age as well," she said with a grin, ignoring the fact that her heart wanted to know him when he was old and gray.

"I'm not sure how well I'll age. My father told me that I could run for Senate and win. That I have the backing of this organization. He told me he would fund the campaign, and his friends have told me they would help me in any way they can."

"You're all over the papers."

"You knew?"

"While you were napping, I was reading. You're one of those rare people who can actually do some good. But that doesn't matter. The only thing that matters is that you want to run. Do you?"

"I've never thought about it. But part of it sounds good to me."

"Well, think about it. Do what makes you happy."

The lights dimmed, signaling that the awards banquet was about to start. They took their seats and listened to the president of the association's speech. She was nervous for him. She had been with Max when he had been honored once, but she hadn't felt much more than minor boredom. Things were so different tonight.

The president finally called Derek's name, highlighting the after-school programs he implemented. How he revitalized a dying economy, how he fought tirelessly for everything he believed in. Derek stood up, looking a little uncomfortable. He was a person who made his voice heard only when it counted.

He stood at the podium, silent for a moment, the most handsome man in the room. Ava's chest filled with admiration and pride as she looked at him. He had this kind of effect on people. He had the power to make anyone he touched adore him.

"I had no idea what I wanted to do with my life when I was a kid," he started. "I was lucky enough to have a man in my life show me that there was more to life than earning money and being powerful and competitive. My uncle taught me that being kind was important, that really listening to people is a sign of respect and that loving unconditionally is hard, but it's the only real way to love something. He also taught me not to go through life doing something for the sake of doing it. Do everything with passion. Do what you love. I am a man who is unconditionally in love with my island. I am passionate about the people who live there. Being their mayor is truly an honor. I don't do what I do for the accolades or awards—I do what I do because knowing the people I serve are taken care of fulfills me in a way that nothing else could. So, I have one big thank-you to the people of Hideaway Island, because without them giving me this job I wouldn't be standing before you as the man I am today. I also want to thank my family, whose love and support is never ending. And to my friends..." Derek looked directly at her. "You push me when I need to be pushed, and listen to me when I need to talk and make me feel alive when my soul is drained. I wouldn't be here without you, either."

He took his eyes off her, and she was glad because she was feeling all sorts of emotions running through her. It was like he was begging her to fall for him. She didn't hear the rest of what he said, but as soon as he came off the stage and sat beside her, she reached out to him, hugging him tightly and as close to her as he could get. "I need you naked as soon as humanly possible."

He pulled away from her slightly, all that pent-up passion and lust that they had been fighting for weeks in his eyes. "Ten more minutes and we can go."

"If we're not back in ten, I'm going to start right here in front of all these people."

It was sixteen minutes before they left the ballroom. Derek's politeness did not allow them to leave before he said his goodbyes and thank-yous.

He took her hand and they walked out, not saying a word to each other, but their footsteps got faster and she felt herself laughing as they started to run. She felt so free in that moment, so happy. She was going to spend the night making love to a man who made her heart beat faster just by looking at her.

It was pouring when they got to the double doors that led outside. "Come on." Derek tugged her hand. "There's an indoor walkway that connects the two hotels."

"Too far."

"Your dress."

"I wore it for you. I'm taking it off for you. I don't give a damn about getting wet."

"Your wish is my command." He pushed open the door and pulled her out into the rain. She was immediately soaked, but she didn't care. She couldn't stop smiling. As they ran through the rain, they accidently bumped into a man who was walking with his head down.

"I'm sorry!"

The man looked up at her, and she froze. She wasn't planning on seeing him again. In fact, she had all but put him out of her mind, but there was Max standing before her, a large designer umbrella over his head and a look of pure annoyance on his face.

It was a moment before he realized it was her, but when

he did, his look of annoyance transformed to one of pure anger. Looking at him now, it was hard for her to remember what it was she loved about him. The only things she wanted from him were loyalty, warmth, that feeling of home whenever she saw him, but she never felt those things. She had fooled herself into thinking they existed with him.

"Max…" She didn't know what to say to him. She had been angry at the betrayal, devastated by it, but she wasn't feeling either of those things in the moment. She had spent an incredible day with a man who treated her like his friend and equal and a priority.

"Who the hell do you think you are?" he started in on her, shocking her with his anger. "Ignoring me for weeks. Me? I own half this state. Do you know how many girls wanted to be you? You send back my gifts. You blocked my calls. You throw me away like some common trash."

"I refuse to let you act like the hurt party. You spent three years lying to me. I was going to spend the rest of my life with you. Being your perfect wife, losing myself in order to make you happy, and you had an entire life that you kept from me."

"My life with them has nothing to do with you."

"It has everything to do with me!" She stepped away from him. "No. I refuse to do this tonight. You will not suck me in. It's over."

Max's eyes flicked over to Derek. It was clear that he hadn't realized who she was with until that moment. "Are you screwing this man? This small-town, self-righteous prig. You're doing this to get back at me."

"I'm not doing anything to get back at you. My life choices ceased being about you the moment I found out about Ingrid."

"You were probably sleeping with him the entire time. That's why you pushed that pathetic little island on me. I should have seen the signs. You're just a whore with a little elegance sprinkled on her."

Derek's arm shot out, and he grabbed the front of Max's shirt and shoved him against the nearest wall, causing his umbrella to tumble to the ground. "You can say whatever the hell you want about me, but you will respect Ava," he said in a quiet voice. "If you call her out of her name again, I will take your head off—do you understand me?"

"Get off me, asshole!"

Derek's forearm pressed a little tighter against Max's neck. "Did you hear what I said?"

"Yes," Max choked out.

"And for the record, Ava would never break her commitment. If you knew anything about her at all, you would have known that." He let go of Max, took her hand and led her inside their hotel. They were both soaked, but unlike a few minutes ago, the giddy joy had faded away. That old hurt that she had thought disappeared had come back, and then there was Derek, now tight with anger. Max had disrespected him and his home on his special night. Ava wasn't sure how she would make it up to him, but she knew she would do everything in her power.

## Chapter 15

Derek lay on his bed, his arm tucked behind his head as he listened to the rain. Ava was silent on the way up to the room. Max was probably the last person she expected to see today. She had been so happy before that moment. He could see the joy in her face, hear it in her laughter. He had felt it, too, because tonight he was finally going to be with her. But then Max showed up, and he immediately saw the change in her expression. Her smile had melted away; the hurt had returned in full force. She said that she had never really loved him, that in her heart she hadn't wanted to marry him. But only someone you deeply loved could hurt you so much.

It had been more than two months now, but two months after three years didn't seem like enough time to heal. It didn't seem like enough time to jump into a new relationship. And if they made love tonight, that's what it would be. He couldn't just be her friend. One night wasn't going to be enough. One hundred nights wouldn't even begin to satisfy him. He wanted all of her. He wanted the world to know that she was his, but he wasn't sure she was ready for all of that. So when they got back to their suite, he walked her to her bedroom door, kissed her still-wet cheek and walked away. It physically hurt him to do so, but it seemed like the honorable thing to do.

He had been lying in bed for the past hour now, unable to sleep. He knew it would be impossible tonight because he couldn't turn off his thoughts of her.

There was a soft knock on his door, but before he could respond Ava walked in. She was in a short, silky white robe, her legs and feet bare. He had been aroused all day, but seeing her walk in, in a state that few got to see her in, turned him on even more.

"Derek?"

"Yeah?"

She sat gingerly at the foot of his bed. "Are you mad at me?"

"No." He shook his head. "Why would you think I was?"

Uncertainty crossed her face. "You didn't make love to me. I thought you wanted to."

"Of course I want to. But I don't want you to have sex with me because you feel obligated. I want you to be with me because you want me and because it will make you feel good, because you can't think of any place else you'd rather be."

"Oh." She stood and in one move dropped her bathrobe to reveal her naked body. "I guess it's a good thing that I do feel that way."

She crawled on to the foot of his bed and ran her palms up his shins. He wanted to reach out to grab her, to pull her on top of him and feel all that beautiful softness, but he was too mesmerized to do anything but watch what she was doing. She bent over and slowly kissed up his legs. He didn't think he had ever been kissed there or if he had, the other woman's kisses just didn't compare with Ava's. Visually she was a gorgeous, erotic picture. Her round behind pointing proudly in the air, her teardrop-shaped breasts bouncing ever so slightly as she moved along his body. She straddled him, lowering her head toward his chest, her lips brushing over his pounding heart before she pressed a kiss there. "I can't tell you how long I've wanted to kiss you all over. Weeks. Months. I used to dream about being here, doing this."

He couldn't resist anymore, and he touched her, gently. It was a struggle because he wanted to grab her, roll her over and push deep inside her, but they had waited too long for that kind of sex. He had promised himself he would take his time, make it last all night. So he settled for stroking his hands down her back and arms. "Let me kiss you," he whispered.

"No." She removed her lips from him and looked him in the eye. "I get too lost kissing you. Not yet."

"Maybe I want you to get lost in my kisses."

"But I'm not ready to give up my turn." She moved to his stomach, peppering little kisses there. He thought it was sweet until she scraped her teeth across his skin. He nearly jumped at the sensation, but he liked it. He liked it even more when she ran her tongue over that spot to soothe it.

He didn't need foreplay with her. He was instantly hard the moment she came into his sight, but she was working hard to make him feel good. Did she know that he hadn't had a truly bad day since she walked into his life?

She hooked her fingers into the waistband of his boxer briefs and began to pull them down. He lifted his hips to assist her. She took them off and flung them behind her, gifting him with a sassy grin. "You don't know how long I've wanted to do that. I've lost two pairs of underwear because of you."

"One pair is in my bedroom. If you come back, I'll be sure to give them to you."

"I'm going to hold you to that." She rested her head on his thigh, her breath tickling his erection. She simply touched it at first, running her fingers lightly over it, causing it to twitch. He sucked in a breath. Her touch was nearly too much to bear.

"Ava, don't play with me. I'm not going to last if you do."

"I have faith in you." She ran her lips up his shaft, stopping periodically to kiss it, but it wasn't those sweet little kisses from before. These were hotter, wetter kisses that were causing him to groan with a mixture of pain and pleasure.

"Ava…"

"Yes?" she asked before opening her warm, wet mouth and enclosing him inside. He nearly bucked off the bed, but she held firm and began to move her mouth on him.

She had an odd combination of sexy confidence and sweet innocence that he found alluring and that he couldn't take his eyes off.

"Let me touch you." He reached for her, pulling her up so that their bodies were aligned. He cupped her breast in his hand, stroking his thumb across her nipple until it was a rock-hard point.

"It's my turn to kiss you all over," he said just before he took her mouth. She moaned and wrapped her arms around him, pushing her breasts against him. He ran his hand down her side, loving the way she felt, the way her waist dipped in, the way her hip gently curved out. And then there was her behind, which seemed to be made for his hand. He deepened the kiss as he pulled her on top of him. He needed to feel her soft weight. He felt grounded with her. Like he could be himself, not the man everyone else expected him to be. Perfect son, perfect nephew, perfect mayor. She was the only person who never expected anything from him, and he appreciated her for that.

She broke the kiss and pulled away. "Where are the condoms?"

"In the nightstand. I didn't get to kiss you all over yet."

"Later. I can't be without you any longer." She pulled a condom out of the box and ripped open the wrapper with her teeth. It was funny and sexy and told him that she wasn't doing this for him, or to forget about Max. She wanted him as much as he wanted her.

"Give it to me." He reached for the condom, but she shook her hands and slid her body down his. She cupped his sack, stroked her hand over his painful erection and did the sexiest thing he had ever been fortunate enough to experience. She slid the condom on with her mouth, all while looking up at him.

"Damn it, Ava."

She just smiled at him and straddled him once again. "Do you feel that, Derek?" She ran his fingers over her folds so he could feel her wetness. "I've never wanted another man as much as I want you." She gave him a mischievous and incredibly sexy smile. "This better be good, because if it's not, I might hurt you."

He laughed, but his laughter faded away as she rose over him and sank all the way down on him. He let out a stream of incoherent words. She was tight and hot, and it was going to take everything in his power to last. She began to move, her hips rocking in a slow, hypnotic rhythm. He forced his eyes to stay open so that he could take in every expression that crossed her face.

She was heavenly to look at, breasts pointed out, head back, eyes closed, mouth open, moans escaping her.

He couldn't just lay there and let her work. He grabbed her arms and pulled her down until her mouth met his. He licked across her lips, begging for entrance, and she allowed it, sucking his tongue deep into her mouth. He grabbed her hips, guiding her down on him. Their pace grew faster, nearly out of control. She broke first and squeezed so tightly around him that it spurred on his own climax. She lay slumped on top of him, her body slightly damp from all the exertion.

"That was great, Mayor Patrick." She sat up. He was still inside her, and the movement made him stir to life again. "That was in the top three sexual experiences of my life." She patted his chest and climbed off him. "I'll be sure to tell all my friends about you."

He grabbed her hand and pulled her back into bed. "Don't be funny right now." He hugged her close to him, and she relaxed into his embrace.

"I'm feeling things," she admitted. "A lot of things and I'm not sure how to handle it."

"Is regret one of them?"

"No."

"Then we're good." He kissed her forehead. "You're not allowed to leave this bed tonight."

"I'm not. It's storming out. I feel safer here with you."

"You really don't like thunderstorms, do you?"

"No. Only Elias knows how much they really bother me. He'll come stay with me if he knows a really bad one is coming and I'll be alone. He switches his shift every time a tropical storm enters the forecast."

"Were you always afraid?"

"No. But I got locked outside of the house during a very bad storm when I was eight. The thunder and wind were so loud that my family didn't hear me knocking. We had an old shed that I took shelter in. I remember it shaking every time it thundered. I was freezing and dripping wet, and I couldn't feel my fingers. I just knew I was going to die that day. But my father came out and found me. I didn't know how he knew I was there, but he opened the shed door and picked me up and took me inside. He wrapped me in a blanket and let me cry for the next two hours. And ever since then, I haven't liked the rain because it reminds me of when I was the most terrified."

He kissed her forehead again. "You should have moved to the desert. Florida is not the best place for you."

"My family is here."

"Where is your mother? I've only met her once. I thought she might have come up to support you during this time."

"I asked her not to come. Being on Hideaway Island makes her incredibly sad. It was a few days after Carlos closed on his house here that my father died. My mother will never remarry. She'll never date again because in her heart she is eternally married to my father."

"It's a sad thing to mourn someone for the rest of your life."

"Yes, but it's a beautiful thing, too. To know that someone loved you that much." She sighed, and he could hear the heavy sadness in her voice. That wasn't his intention tonight. Tonight he only wanted her to be happy. "She spends most of her time in Costa Rica now. Carlos bought her and her sisters a huge house. There's four of them and my grandmother. All widowed or divorced. They are hysterical together. Like a bunch of beautiful, bickering peacocks. My mother needs to be with them. They were the reason she got out of bed again after my father died. My sadness wouldn't have been good for her."

"I understand."

"Now it's your turn to tell me something about yourself."

"What do you want to know? You know almost everything about me."

"I want to know about all the women before me."

"We've just made love and you want to talk about other women? It's weird."

"I know. I'm still feeling too many things. I need to think about something else."

He sighed, realizing he would do nearly anything to make her happy. "What do you want to know?"

"Humor me. Do you have a type?"

"I guess you could say that."

"Am I it?"

"No."

"I'm not sure if I should be offended by that or not." Thunder sounded around them, and she pushed herself closer to him. He rubbed her back in slow circles, trying to soothe away her fear. "Keep talking to me."

"I've dated older women."

"Mommy issues?"

"No! They weren't much older than me. Maybe ten years at the most. For the past six years, I've only dated divorcées who already had their children and wanted no part of marriage."

"You don't want to get married one day?"

"I didn't. Marriage wasn't something I saw for myself. Falling in love seemed terrible." He realized that he was speaking in the past tense.

*Didn't.*

*Wasn't.*

But he didn't feel like that anymore. If being with Ava was anything at all what it was like to be married, then he could see himself there. In fact, it would be hard to imagine life alone after being with her.

"But your grandmother was deeply in love with your grandfather. And then there are your aunts. They married incredible men."

"Then there's my parents. I'm a bastard, born to a mistress that my father didn't even bother trying to hide. They raged at each other. He would scream. She would smash things. They were the definition of dysfunction, and I didn't want that. If love could make you act like that, I wanted to avoid it. So I avoided women like you. Beautiful, young ones with hopes of marriage in their eyes and biological clocks that were ticking. And because I'll never forget my father cursing my mother for trying to get him stuck. Stuck with her and an extra kid that he never wanted."

"I'm sorry." She cupped his face and kissed him softly on the lips.

"It's true, though. That's why she got pregnant, and if I were my father I might feel the same way. Stuck with a child I didn't want. Stuck co-parenting with a woman I didn't love that much in the first place."

"I hate that your parents did that to you. I hate that they made you see love in such an ugly way."

"I'm fine now," he said truthfully. He was fine because he had met her. It was like some heavy gate had lifted, and now where there had been nothing, there was a lifetime of possibilities.

He kissed her lips lightly and then moved down to her chest, his lips brushing over the curve of her breast. "It's my turn to kiss you all over."

"Good." She gave a dreamy sigh. "Because I won't be happy unless you make love to me all night."

Ava looked up at Derek that next afternoon. They were standing on her front porch back on Hideaway Island after lingering in bed all that morning. She had missed the island immediately when the ferry set sail, but now that they were back she was feeling a little sad. Their first night was over. They could never relive it or redo it. Freezing time wasn't an option. They could only move forward and she knew moving forward would mean she would have to make decisions. Big ones. Part of her wished that she could just stay on this island inside its comforting protective bubble forever, but she knew that could never be.

"I have to go into city hall for a few hours to get some work done," he said to her as he wrapped his arms around her waist.

"I thought you worked mostly from home."

"I do, but I won't be able to get a damn thing done knowing that you're within walking distance."

She had lost count of how many times they had made love. Delicious sleepy sex, fast, hot, explosive sex. Comfortable sex, as if they had known each other's bodies for years. She had never been with anyone like that. It was like he had stripped away all these layers she was unaware of and all that was left was a raw, goopy mess that was more vulnerable than ever before.

"Can I come over when I'm done? I'll bring dinner. Or I can take you out. Wherever you want to go. Even that fancy place that requires men to wear ties and suit jackets."

"You really must be impressed with my bedroom skills if you're willing to wear a tie again."

He brushed a kiss across her lips. "I'm impressed with you period. But I do have to admit that what you did to me in the shower this morning made me go blind for a few minutes."

She laughed, and he held her a little closer. She found that she didn't want him to go. They had spent the last twenty-four hours together, but she still wanted more. It was slightly troubling. "I wouldn't make you wear a tie two days in a row. Let's stay in. I can cook for you."

"Not tonight." He kissed her again. "Relax for the rest of the day. I'm feeling the need to spoil you, but I'm not sure how."

"You being you is enough for me."

He looked at her for a long moment, and he looked at her so tenderly that she wasn't sure her heart could take it. "I have to go." He stepped away from her. "If I kiss you again, I won't be able to stop."

"Go to work, Derek."

He nodded and walked off her porch just as her sister-in-law's car pulled into her driveway.

"Hello, Derek," Virginia said happily as she took her daughter out of the car.

"Hey!" He walked over to her and lifted Bria out of her arms. "Hello, little one. You're getting gorgeous like your mama."

"She looks like her father, and you know it."

"But she has your eyes, and you have the kind of eyes a man could get lost in."

"Oh, smooth. Very, very smooth," Virginia said. Ava could tell she was flattered.

"Have a nice visit with your aunt." He gave Bria a little kiss on her cheek and handed her back to Virginia.

"That man," Virginia said as soon as he had pulled away. "I came here to talk about him." She reached into her diaper bag, pulled out a page from the newspaper and handed it to Ava.

There was a long article about the event last night, including photographs. There was one of Derek onstage looking so handsome in his tux. There was one with him and his father with the governor of Florida. But the biggest picture there was of him and her. It was a close-up of them, their foreheads pressed together. His eyes were closed. Hers were open, and she was looking at him with a mix of love and awe and pride.

Her stomach clenched. Even if she couldn't admit it to herself, her feelings for him were written all over her face, and now the whole world could see it.

"I've never seen you look more beautiful," Virginia said softly.

"This isn't good," Ava moaned.

"No. It's amazing. Derek is a wonderful man."

"Two months ago I was ready to spend the rest of my life with another man. It's just too soon to fall in love again."

"So you admit you're in love with him?"

"No. I don't know what I am. Derek is sexy and brilliant and caring. Everyone he meets falls in love with him. I could be like every other person in this town who has fallen into his charming trap."

"But unlike every other person in town, Derek chooses to spend every ounce of his free time with you. You do realize that the entire island has been talking about you two."

"I'm trying not to think about it. We ran into Max last night," she admitted to Virginia. "He's furious with me. He accused me of cheating on him with Derek."

"You mean to tell me that the guy with the secret family had the nerve to accuse you of being unfaithful?"

"That made Derek angry, and he shoved Max against a wall and cut off his airway."

"What!"

"Did I mention it was pouring? I knew I should've told Derek to stop, but it was incredibly sexy."

"What happened after that?"

"We went back to our suite and had sex about a thousand times."

Virginia glanced at her now eight-month-old daughter and covered her ears. "How was the sex? Derek looks… I don't know. He just seems like he's one of those men who puts in one hundred and ten percent at everything he does."

"Virginia." She sighed, thinking back to last night. "There are no words. He smiles at me and my underwear slips off. I have never had sex like that and feel like it would be impossible for me to have that with another man. Being with him is an experience that every woman should have at least once."

"He's serious about you, Ava. Derek has never been seen publicly with another woman, and he's gone everywhere with you. That gala last night was hugely important to him, and he chose to take you. He's telling the world that he's proud to have you, that he's crazy about you."

"I've been offered a job," she blurted out. "A big one. It's a dream job, and I would be crazy to turn it down."

"It's a job you couldn't do here on this tiny island, I'm assuming."

"No. I would be based in Miami, but I would be traveling to Europe a lot."

"And you turned down a big promotion and quit your job for Max, and you don't want to do the same for Derek."

She shook her head. "It's not about giving things up for Derek. It's about giving up on myself. Look at you. You're living your dream, and you did it without giving up anything for a man."

"No, but he was willing to give it all up for me. Have you talked to Derek? There might be a way to make it work."

"It's too soon to talk about anything. We only made love for the first time last night."

"Really? Your brother was convinced you two have been going at it for weeks."

"We haven't. But we should've been. I've been missing out on a lot," she joked.

Virginia sighed. "I wish this was easier. We all hated Max. We love Derek, and we just want you to be happy."

"Why didn't anyone tell me that they hated him? Not a single one of you ever said a word about it. Well, Elias did, but he never likes any of the men I date."

"He treated you like a princess, and we thought you loved him. It's not our place to tell you how to live your life."

"No, but you could have said something."

"I'm saying something now. We all like Derek. Even Elias. If he makes you happy, you should do what it takes to keep him. Some other woman might snatch him up—hell, I might even go for him."

"Hey! You're married to my brother."

"Oh, that's right, and I'm crazy in love with him, too." She shrugged. "Oh well. I figured we should keep him in the family. Come on—let's go inside. I think we both could use some wine."

## *Chapter 16*

The next evening Derek pulled into his driveway to see Ava just getting out of her car. She was wearing heels and a fitted cream-colored dress. She held a designer bag in her hand, and he realized that she looked like her old self. The woman who was engaged to be married to another man. The only difference that remained was her hair. It was in the soft waves that he had grown ridiculously fond of.

"Hey!" She smiled at him, seeming genuinely happy to see him. "Come help me carry these groceries inside."

He walked over and kissed her, lingering just a little longer than he should. "You look beautiful. How was your day?" He took two large bags out of the car, trying not to read too much into her change back to her more buttoned-up attire. He was hoping she stayed on the island, but he couldn't ignore that she had received that job offer. She said her stay here was just an extended vacation. That she had to get back to real life. It was selfish to want her to have a real life here, but he had been selfless his entire life. He wanted to be selfish when it came to her.

"Thank you. I got this dress when I was shopping with your grandmother. In fact, I was with her again today. We had lunch with a bunch of her friends at the community center."

"You've been down there a lot."

"I know. I love older women. There's so much life experience there. It's Nancy's birthday tomorrow. I'm going to make a cake and some hors d'oeuvres. You should stop by the center. It will make her day."

"Okay, I will."

They went directly to the kitchen and started unpacking the bags. Ava had gotten a lot of things for the party, and he stepped aside and watched her organize it all the way she liked it. He was happy to stand there and have her order him around.

"I'm going to cook for you tonight. Garlic rice and shrimp or *arroz al ajillo* as my mother would call it. Any objections?" she asked as she started to pull out the ingredients she needed for the dish.

"Yes, I have one objection."

"What?" Her eyes widened a bit.

He grabbed her by the hips and pulled her close to him. "I haven't gotten the chance to really kiss you in ten hours." He ran his tongue across her lower lip and felt her body go slack against his. He'd had to leave her early that morning. Founder's day was quickly approaching. And since this year's festivities were larger, there was even more planning that needed to be done.

The kiss immediately turned hot, and soon he found himself hiking up her dress and pushing her against the wall.

"Ouch!" Ava flinched.

Derek backed away immediately. "Did I hurt you?"

"Not directly. Remember when things got a little carried away last night after dinner and we couldn't make it to the bedroom?"

"Yeah."

"I'm not sure coffee tables are meant for such vigorous activity."

"I'm sorry, baby. Why didn't you tell me you were uncomfortable?"

"I wasn't." She ran his hand over the back of his head. "Couldn't you tell?"

He nodded. "I got it. Only make love to you on soft things. Beds, couches, chaise lounges."

"Grass, sand, the backseat of a car." She nodded with a smile. "I am fond of the shower, too. Maybe once my back quits aching we can try that again."

"I'm sorry." He gave her a slow kiss. "I can't control myself around you."

"I can't control myself either." She shut her eyes and rested her head on his shoulder. "Maybe you shouldn't sleep over tonight."

"You don't want to have sex? We don't have to. This is not only about sex for me."

"I do want to have sex tonight. I just want you to go home after."

"Why? Are you expecting company?"

"No, you jackass." Her expression grew serious. "I don't want to leave this island with another broken heart."

That caused him to stiffen. "I'm not going to hurt you."

"No, but the more time I spend with you the more attached I'm becoming. I didn't plan for this, Derek. I came to this island two months ago expecting to leave married to someone else. Only that never happened."

"Are you still in love with Max?"

"No. Of course not," she said and he believed her, but the pit in his stomach didn't ease. He knew he may not be able to have her forever but he wanted all of her for as long as he could. "I turned down a promotion for him and ended up giving up my career to be with him. I didn't feel right doing it, but I did it to make him happy. I'm not sure I could do it again. I was handed an opportunity that I could never dream of, and I just can't turn it away. But I can't turn you away, either. You're all I think about."

"And you don't want to think about me anymore?"

"I just want to be able to leave this island. This is your home. These are your people. Your life is meant to be here, but mine isn't."

"And you think not sleeping with me at night is going to accomplish that?"

"No." She looped her arms around him and kissed him with all the passion of before. "But it's the only thing I can bear doing right now." She unbuttoned his jeans and slipped her hand inside, finding his just-forming erection and stroking it until it was fully hard and ready for her. "It not dark yet. Let's see how many times you can make love to me until it is."

The private dining room they had reserved at the community center looked lovely. Ava had ordered fresh flowers that morning. Beautiful purple lilies from one of the local women who had just opened a floral design studio downtown. She had strung white paper lanterns from the ceiling and placed white candles in all different shapes and sizes in clear white vases. It was elegant and whimsical, and when Nancy had walked in the room, her eyes lit with surprise and she started to cry. It made Ava feel better than she had in years. Well, with the exception of when she was with Derek. She still felt some guilt when it came to him. He seemed fine when she had kissed him goodbye last night. But she knew she had hurt him when she told him that she didn't want to grow any more attached to him. But it was the truth. What kind of woman would she be if she derived all her happiness from a man? She needed to know herself before she would completely give her heart away again.

"My dear girl." Nanny came over to her and looped her arm through hers. She was wearing a pair of fitted white pants and a patterned blush-colored blouse. The woman was the definition of style and grace, and Ava was really starting to love her. "This room looks spectacular and Nancy looks so incredibly happy. I've been worried about her since her husband passed. They were married for sixty-two years."

"I noticed some sadness around her," she said, looking at the woman, who was now laughing as she held a glass of champagne in her hand. "You only turn eighty once."

"How did you pull this off so quickly? You must have stayed up all night doing this."

"She made me help." She heard Derek's voice from behind her, and her heart immediately started to beat faster.

She couldn't prevent the smile that spread across her face when she saw him. He wore a fitted rust-colored T-shirt and some blue jeans that fit him perfectly, forming to the powerful thighs she loved to run her hands over. "You came."

"You asked me to. Hello, Nanny." He quickly kissed his grandmother's cheek before he turned his attention to Ava and gave her a kiss that lasted just a little too long for public. Derek was the king of lingering kisses. He gave the kind of kisses she was sure she would never get tired of. "Hello, you."

"Hello." She hoped she wasn't blushing. It was clear he wasn't attempting to distance himself from her and that they were an item, but she wasn't sure what they were. Was he her boyfriend? She had had boyfriends before, but none of them made her feel quite this way.

"Did you decorate this place by yourself?" he asked her, looking around.

"I did."

"So this is where you were going when I saw you leave at seven this morning?"

"Yes."

"She's a very talented girl," Nanny said.

"I know," Derek replied. "She impresses me every day. I thought you were having cake and a few snacks. You really went all out."

"It wasn't much. It gave me something to do. I need to feel useful again."

"You're always useful and wanted here," Derek said, looking her directly in the eye. She knew they were no longer talking about the party. He had never directly said he didn't want her to go. He never would, but she knew what he was getting at, and it made her heart swell a bit.

Nanny made a soft noise. "There's a job opening here," she said. "We need an activities director. You've taken us shopping, organized a party and are an excellent bridge player. You could do the job. We could recommend you. My grandson is mayor. I think he has some pull here." She winked at him.

"Ava has been offered a very big job in Miami," Derek said, his voice flat, which meant that he had very strong feelings about it, but he didn't want to let on.

"You're leaving?" Nanny looked dismayed, and that simultaneously warmed Ava's heart and made her feel terrible.

"The job doesn't start for another two months or so. I haven't given my final answer yet." She wasn't sure why she had said that. She had made up her mind. She was going to take the job because another opportunity like this wasn't going to come her way.

"Well, you can be the activities director until you go. And we can find you other things to do around the island—can't we, Derek? I know you need help planning the founder's day dance. Look how Ava decorated this room. I think she'll do an incredible job. Won't you, dear?"

"Um, yes sure." Nanny was deciding for her. It seemed foolish to protest.

"Tell her what the theme is, Derek."

"A night in Paris."

"I can do that. I still have stuff left over from my wedding that we couldn't return. I can donate it."

"That will be perfect." Derek nodded. "The town will greatly appreciate that."

He was a little cooler with her, more professional. He was speaking to her like he was the mayor and she was just some ordinary citizen. She could take his anger more than she could take his distance. But distance was what they needed; it was what she had asked for. It was the only way she could escape the island with her heart intact. Still, she found herself grabbing his hand and slipping her fingers between his. "Come have something to eat, Mr. Mayor. I'll fix you a plate."

# *Chapter 17*

$A$va was sitting on Derek's front steps when he pulled into his driveway the next night. He hadn't seen her since the day before at the party, where she had served as hostess. She was dressed to the nines again in a sea-foam-green sheath dress and nude stilettos. She was painfully beautiful, but she wasn't his Ava in those clothes. She was the Ava she presented to the world.

"Hello," he said to her.

"Hello, Mayor Ass Face," she responded.

He was taken aback by her response for a moment, but he realized that she was angry with him. "Glad to see we're being mature this evening."

"Don't you dare get polite and formal on me, Derek Patrick." She stood up, wagging her finger at him. "Instead of speaking to me like a man, you're sulking like a little boy. I let you see a side of me that no one else ever has. You know me more intimately than anyone else. You're my best friend, damn it! You don't get to go cold on me."

"I'm not going cold on you. I'm giving you the space you asked for. You need to get used to it, because space is all we're going to have when you leave the island in a couple of months."

"I asked for a little space at night. Eight hours to be alone with my thoughts. I can't be alone with my thoughts of you because when I'm with you, you're all I think about. When I wake up in the morning you're the first person I want to see—you're what I look forward to each day. You have this crazy effect on me and I don't know why and it scares the hell out of me."

"You think I don't feel the same way? I have to force myself to go to work every morning because spending the day with you is all I want to do. I'm taking myself to city hall and spending hours in my office at a desk, which I hate, because I know if I'm anywhere near you, I can't control myself. Do you realize how huge of an issue this is for me? Work was my life. Making furniture and running this town was my life. And then you came along out of the blue and changed everything. You don't think I'm scared? You don't think I think about my feelings for you and feel choked?"

He was in love with her; for the first time in his life he was really truly in love. He had been trying to deny his feelings, to skate around them, but he loved her, and he couldn't stomach the thought of losing her so soon.

They were quiet for a moment, just staring at each other.

A car pulled up behind him, breaking their spell. At first he didn't recognize the flashy, brand-new candy-apple-red sports car, but then he saw his mother get out. She was wearing oversize sunglasses, a short sundress and high-heeled gladiator sandals. His stomach rolled with apprehension, which wasn't the way he should feel about his mother. He should be happy to see her, and he felt guilty about it.

"Hi, Mom. I wasn't expecting you."

"I know." She gave him a bright smile. "I don't need an

excuse to see my baby boy, do I?" She turned back toward her car. "I almost forgot. I brought you a little present. It's a pie! You like pie, don't you, love?"

"Yeah, Mom."

Ava came down the steps and touched his arm.

"Mom, I don't think you've met Ava yet."

"No, I haven't." His mother's eyes turned critical, and she looked Ava up and down. "You certainly are a beauty. Maybe a little too beautiful. I was too beautiful when I was your age. Only I preferred to dress with a little more…flair."

Derek wasn't sure if his mother was taking a shot at Ava, but it seemed like she was. He immediately grew protective. "Ava's a fashion buyer. Maybe she should take you shopping. You might learn something new." His words were uncharacteristic. He always was respectful of his elders, especially his mother, even when it was impossible. But he needed to stop her in her tracks. She would tear any woman down she felt was a threat to her. He had seen her do it before.

His mother took note and straightened a bit. "I didn't mean anything by that, sweetie. You know how your mama is."

"I do."

"I was hoping we could have a little chat." She looked at Ava, clearly wanting her to leave.

"You two should have dinner," Ava said to him. "It's in your oven. I made seafood lasagna and salad. There's fresh garlic bread on the counter. I'll give you some privacy."

"You cooked?" He frowned at her, not knowing that she had gone through all that trouble for him.

She nodded. "I wanted to."

"You aren't going anywhere." He looked over to his mother. "Package deal. Take it or leave it."

She seemed surprised with his answer, but she nodded.

"I would be happy to join you for dinner. Thank you for the invitation."

They all went inside, the tension thick around them. He could see that Ava had straightened up again. He never expected her to cook and clean for him; in fact, it made him a little uncomfortable. He wanted to be the one to take care of her, not the other way around.

"I wish you hadn't gone through all this trouble," he said once they walked into the kitchen. It smelled heavenly. She had placed a small red-checked tablecloth on his table. There was a little vase with wildflowers in it and a single flickering candle. She was a details person, while he was a big-picture man. But he was realizing that it was the little details that really made life special.

"It wasn't trouble. I like doing it. In my old life I was treated like a delicate flower. I never had to cook or clean or do anything for myself because there was always a servant to do it for me. But I like to be able to cook dinner. I like to make the house pretty. I don't do these things for you. I do them for myself."

"Oh, honey, why?" His mother shook her head in disbelief. "You were engaged to a billionaire. You did good. I don't know why you gave all of that up. I know my son is a catch, but, sweetie, you were at the top. I still can't fathom why you would let him go."

"He wasn't the man I thought he was."

"Cheater?" She nodded sympathetically. "It stings, but sometimes you have to put up with it to get what you need in the long run. Men that powerful and successful just cannot keep it in their pants. They want to share it with the entire word."

"I'm nobody's second place," Ava said before she turned away to put the garlic bread in the oven.

Derek suppressed a smile. Max was a fool. With each passing day he was more and more grateful for that.

"Mom, can I offer you something to drink?" He opened the refrigerator and saw that Ava had stocked it for him. "I have lemonade, tea and bottled water."

"Do have any wine? Maybe something a little harder than that?"

He did, but he purposely hadn't offered it to her. His mother wasn't a problem drinker, but he knew the alcohol made her a little freer with her emotions, and when she got that way his father always came up. He was going to come up tonight. He knew that's why she was there.

"Red or white?" Ava asked when he didn't answer at first. "White goes with seafood, but we don't follow those fussy rules here."

"I'll take red then. My boyfriend is a bit of a wine snob. Won't drink anything American. Speaking of that, you didn't say anything about my new car," she said as she sat down at the table. "He bought it for me. Isn't it the sexiest car you've ever seen?"

"It's nice, Mom."

"When are you going to buy me a car?" Ava asked him with a smile.

He stepped forward and pressed his mouth to hers. "Never," he said, speaking into her lips. "I wouldn't want you to think I was buying your love."

"It's free," she said, giving him a soft peck. "Pour your mother some wine."

Ava served them. The meal was beautiful to look at and tasted even better. Even his mother, who ruthlessly watched her figure, was eating with gusto.

"Everything is great, Ava."

"Thank you."

"It really is," his mother said, taking another bite. "I had salmon and spinach lasagna at some fancy restaurant in Miami. Yours is almost as good. You should try that recipe for Derek. I'm sure he would like it."

"Derek hates salmon. He got food poisoning from it."

"You did? Was this recently?"

"No, Mom. When I was fifteen, I ended up in the hospital for two days."

"Oh." She shrugged. "I really didn't remember that."

Of course she didn't. His mother had taken him to the hospital, but had left the island to be with one of her boyfriends, and his uncle and aunt had taken care of him for the rest of the month. "Did you want to talk about something, Mom?"

"Not really. I just wanted to see how the gala was. I thought you weren't going. I offered to go with you."

"I changed my mind."

"I saw the article in the paper. You looked amazing. I didn't think you had that much fashion sense."

"I don't. That was Ava's doing."

"And did she buy you the shirt you're wearing? It's new and clean and fits you."

He looked over at her. "Did you? I couldn't remember buying this."

"Yes. I bought a few things for you," she said quietly. "I was hoping you wouldn't notice."

"Why did you do that?"

"Because you needed them, and I know it wouldn't occur to you to go shopping."

"This I approve of. His father was a much better dresser. Did you meet him the other day?"

"I did. Derek looks just like him."

"I know. He's a proud papa. He let himself have his picture snapped with you. Anyone who looks at the two of you will know you're related."

"He didn't try to hide it. He introduced me as his son."

"Was his wife there? How did the old hag respond to that?"

"He was there alone, Mom."

"Trouble in paradise?" Derek saw a little gleam in her eye that he didn't like.

"No. They aren't going to get divorced. She's his partner."

She was quiet for a long moment, a slight frown creasing her brow. "What did you talk about?"

"There's talk of me running for Senate. Dad said he would fund my campaign."

"Are you going to run? You should run," she said with breathless excitement. "I'll help you campaign. I'll go all around the state with you."

She was hoping to run into Victor. She wasn't even trying to avoid her obsession with him. They had been apart for more than twenty years and yet none of it had dulled for her. Nanny told him that she had always been a bit of a wild child, but she had been sweet and thoughtful, too. But the day she had met his father she had completely changed. "I wasn't planning to run."

"Oh." The disappointment was clear in her voice. "Did you talk about anything else?"

"I'm sure they talked about me," Ava said, getting up and taking their plates.

"We did," he admitted.

"Bet he warned you that I might be a gold digger."

"He did. I set him straight."

"I've heard it before," she said with sadness in her voice. "Social climber, ice queen. I even once got mistaken for a high-class prostitute. I was incredibly offended until he offered me thirty-thousand dollars for one night. Then it was kind of flattering."

She broke the tension with her statement, and Derek found himself laughing for the first time that day. "I would have run my fist through that guy's head."

"I know you would have. Anyone want dessert? I have chocolate cake from the Milo's Bakeshop. Milo gave it to me for free and said to congratulate you on your award."

"He recognized you?"

She nodded as she removed the cake from the box. "I think the big picture of us in the paper tipped him off." Derek hadn't read the article, but he had looked at the picture a couple dozen times. He hadn't seen a photographer around them in that moment but whoever they were had captured something special between them. He would keep the paper forever just because of that one photograph.

"How big of a piece do you want, Derek? This cake looks delicious."

"I bought pie for you," his mother said. "Have some of that."

"Okay, Mom. I will."

But Ava didn't cut into the pie. She continued to slice the cake and set it before him. He looked up at her, questioning. He had preferred the cake, but he hadn't wanted to intentionally hurt his mother's feelings for no good reason.

"It's cherry pie," she said softly.

"Oh."

"What's wrong with the pie I bought?"

"Nothing, except that if your son eats it, his lips will swell and he'll break out in a rash."

"You're allergic to cherries?"

"Yes."

"Since when?"

"Since always, Mom." He felt himself grow weary then. She knew nothing about him. They might as well be strangers.

"Maybe if you were more interested in your son and less in the man you created him with, you might learn these things."

"Ava," he warned, but she was right. His mother hadn't come here to see him, but rather to pump him for information about his father.

"Maybe I shouldn't have come over here tonight." His

mother stood in a huff. "Let me know when you're free to talk in private."

She stormed off, and Derek was relieved to see her go.

"I'm sorry," Ava said, coming over to him. "I couldn't take it anymore. I know she's your mother and that you love her, but how could she not know you? How could she care about him more?"

He wrapped his arms around her waist and rested his head against her stomach. "Don't apologize. It's who she is. I'm used to it."

"You deserve to be loved, Derek. For who you are and for no other reason." She kissed the top of his head.

He *was* loved like that, and she was the person who loved him. She replaced his clothing and stocked his refrigerator and knew what he was allergic to. She didn't have to tell him that she loved him. He knew it in his gut. He felt it in everything she did, and now it was his job to prove to her that he felt exactly the same way.

A couple of weeks later Ava watched Derek get out of bed, naked as the day he was born and head to the bathroom. The lights were dim, but she could still see his perfectly formed nude body clearly. They had just finished making love for the second time that night. Keeping her distance from him at night wasn't working. She tried. Some nights she sent him home. Some nights she left his bed in the middle of the night and retreated to hers, feeling cold and alone. But there were some nights like tonight that she just couldn't leave him.

She had started her job at the senior center. It was just four days a week for five hours, just enough to get her out of the house and interacting with the people of the island. She found herself organizing group outings. Last week they had gone to the beach. Two days ago she had commandeered the community trolley and had bused a group of fifteen seniors to Carlos's house. Virginia had given a painting lesson to the seniors right there on the beach. Her sister-in-law didn't bat a lash when she told her that she had taken the job at the senior center. Her brothers were a different story. They both acted like she had gone off the deep end. They both still acted princess unable to do meaningful work, but she really enjoyed being with the seniors. She enjoyed planning things. She liked taking them shopping and helping them pick out clothes they felt good in. Seeing them smile made her feel good. This job gave her the kind of satisfaction that she had never gotten as a buyer. She looked forward to going to work, and when she wasn't there, she was with Derek. Helping him with his business, fielding calls and taking orders. He even trusted her with the key to his showroom in town when he had a meeting he couldn't get out of. She had recently sold four pieces to some tourists. He offered to pay her commission, but she didn't want anything from him.

Max had given her expensive baubles, gowns and possessions that in the long run didn't mean anything. But Derek gave her his time, attention and affection, and sometimes she felt spoiled by it.

Derek walked back in the room, his face serious as he crawled back in bed. He gathered her close and brushed the hair off her forehead. She had noticed a slight change in him since the night they had dinner with his mother. Only she didn't know if the change had anything to do with his mother or the big argument they had before she arrived. He had been a little quieter, a little more introspective than usual. They had said some deep words to each other. Words they had never mentioned after that night. Ava had been so annoyed with his selfish mother that rehashing it didn't cross her mind.

"What's the matter?"

"I have something to tell you, and I'm not sure how you're going to respond."

"If you tell me you're cheating on me, I will grab the heaviest thing I can find and do you great bodily harm."

He flashed a quick smile. "I would never cheat. I've seen you enraged before."

"What is it, honey?" She stroked his cheek with the backs of her fingers.

"The condom broke."

"I'm on birth control, and I get tested yearly. The last time was right after I found out about Max. You're the only one I've been with since."

"I've been tested, too. That's not the issue. I was thinking more about pregnancy."

"You don't have to worry about that." She was quiet for a long moment. "But what if I weren't on birth control? What if I did get pregnant? What would you do?"

"I think you would already know what I would do. I definitely wouldn't want my child growing up like I did."

"I'm not like your mother. Our baby would be the center of my life."

"I know, but it's important for me for my child to grow up in a stable two-parent home. I want the mother of my child to be my wife. I would want a family."

"But we're living in modern times. Two people can co-parent without marriage. They can raise a well-adjusted, happy child. It's not fair to the parents to be stuck in a loveless marriage just because they had a child."

"You asked me what *I* would do if *you* were pregnant. I would ask you to be my wife. I know our marriage wouldn't be loveless. I know I wouldn't feel stuck. You don't have to ask me what I would do. The question is what would you do?"

## Chapter 18

Founder's day celebration week had finally come. It took months of planning, but it all had come together. The parade had taken place earlier in the day, and the entire town came out. All of them smiling, happy to be there and celebrate their small island town. There were art exhibits and shows. Every artisan in town displayed their work. There were food vendors and souvenir sellers and the biggest farmer's market their town had ever seen. It was a good week, and it wasn't over until tonight. The dinner dance was the event that everyone looked forward to all year. Ava was only supposed to do the decorations, but as the week had passed he found that he was turning over more and more responsibilities to her. She had become a fixture in his life. In this town. She took over the organizational aspects of his business. She answered his emails, took down his orders, set up a dedicated phone line to separate his business and personal calls. She anticipated his needs before he knew he needed them, and he wanted to find a way to repay her. But nothing in the world seemed good enough.

She was still attempting to keep a small amount of distance between them. A month had passed since they had fought about it, since she'd told him that she was scared of how much she felt for him.

Yes, it had only been a few months, but when it was right it was right, and they owed it to themselves to try.

He walked into the event expecting to see some cute Paris theme, but he was blown away. The room had been transformed into something magical. It was dark in there, the walls draped in silky blue fabric. There was no light coming from the fixtures, but the room was illuminated with thousands of little twinkling lights. And there were street lamps. Full-size wrought iron street lamps. Derek didn't know where they had come from, but there were a dozen of them lining what looked like a stone path that led to the dance floor and stage. In one corner of the room there were benches and live bushes full of fresh flowers. On every table there were miniature Eiffel Towers surrounded by lush violet flowers, and on each place setting there were little Tiffany-blue boxes.

"Derek," Nanny said as she touched his shoulder. She was dressed for the evening in an elegant royal-blue cocktail dress. Her long white hair was swept up.

"Hello, Nanny." He kissed her cheek. "You look beautiful."

"Thank you. You're looking handsome yourself."

"Ava," he explained. "I cannot believe what she did to this room." He took it all in for a long moment before speaking again. "I don't know how she pulled it together in such a short amount of time."

"She's incredible."

"She is."

"You're in love with her."

"I am," he admitted aloud for the first time.

"Have you told her?"

"No."

"Why not? It's obvious to the rest of the world."

"She's going to leave here."

"That job offer in Miami? No." She shook her head. "You two have gotten so much closer this past month. She's part of our family."

"I overheard her on the phone last night. They want to her to come to Miami to discuss the job. They are giving her a chance at a career she's always wanted. I'm not sure this island is enough for her."

"She's not leaving. I know in my gut she's going to stay. She has to."

"Who has to?"

Derek turned around to see Ava standing there. He was breathless and speechless and amazed by her again. She was a throwback to another time in her strapless ivory cocktail dress. There were tiny pink roses embroidered on to the tulle skirt and on her feet she wore baby-pink heels. Ava could be incredibly sexy, but tonight she looked perfectly sweet.

He grabbed her by the waist and pulled her into a long kiss. He hadn't seen her since that morning. He had wanted her with him for some of the founder's day activities, but he now understood where she had been spending most of her time.

"Derek." She smacked his shoulder. "You can't kiss me like that in front of your grandmother."

"That was a hello-I-missed-you-this-place-looks-phenomenal kiss."

"You like it?"

"I love it. I'm just not sure how we'll be able to pull anything like this off in the future."

"That's easy," Nanny said. "Ava will just have to plan

it again next year. This is spectacular, dear. Truly spectacular."

"Thank you. I appreciate that."

"Derek, I came to ask you if you have heard from your mother today."

"She might have tried to call, but I have been so busy today I haven't been able to check my messages. Why?"

"She called me three times. I tried to call her back, but she didn't pick up." Worry crossed Nanny's face, and immediately a thick knot formed in Derek's stomach.

He hadn't spoken to his mother since the night she stormed out of his house. He didn't get along with her, but he could still be worried about her. She could be selfish and self-centered, but in a way she was fragile. And the last thing he wanted was for her to be unhappy.

"Maybe I should go check on her."

"No," Nanny said firmly. "She's my child. Not yours. I'll check on her. This town is your baby, and your place is here."

Nanny left them alone, and Ava wrapped her arms around Derek and rested her cheek against his chest. He ran his hands over her smooth bare shoulders, taking comfort from the feel of her skin and growing slightly aroused, remembering how good her nude body felt beneath his hands. "What can I say to take your mind off your mother?"

"My mind is on you right now. Have I told you that you are the most beautiful woman in all of Hideaway Island tonight?"

"Just tonight?" She grinned up at him.

"Every night. You really outdid yourself tonight, Ava. The entire town is going to be talking about this night for years."

"I love this island. I wanted to do something nice for the people here."

"I'm just afraid to ask how you afforded all of this. We didn't give you that big of a budget."

"A lot of the stuff for my wedding was not returnable, but we were allowed to exchange some things. The blue draperies and the lights and the favors."

"There are street lamps and an entire park in here. You did more than exchange."

"I spent three years with Maxime. I had more diamonds than one girl could wear in four lifetimes. I sold the necklace he gave me on our first anniversary. It covered everything and then some. I could buy a car if I wanted."

"It must have been some necklace."

"I didn't like it. It was just too much."

"That makes me feel better about the gift I got you." He slipped a cameo necklace out of his pocket. "I know it's a little old-fashioned, but I saw this and thought of you." It was vintage cameo in a gold setting with twelve tiny diamonds.

"Derek…it's…so perfect."

He placed it on her. As he was clasping it, he heard voices coming from the hallway. "It sounds like our guests are arriving."

"Our guests?"

"Yes, this is our night and our town and our people. I wouldn't be here without you."

Ava had wanted this night to be perfect. She had spent six months planning her wedding as if it were a full-time job. It was her dream since she was a little girl to have one perfect night here on Hideaway Island. She wanted to be in a beautiful dress dancing with a handsome man. She pictured herself being happy. She had that tonight. She got to dance with Derek in a beautiful dress made by a woman who owned a shop on this island. But it wasn't the first perfect night she'd had here. She'd had many perfect nights with Derek, but she could tell by looking at him that this night wasn't perfect for him. He had been gracious and smiling. He greeted every person at the dance by name. He enjoyed champagne and had lively conversations, but she could tell he was worried. He had glanced at his phone more than once. He had never done that. He was always in the present. Every dinner they had shared, every night they were together he turned all his attention to her. But tonight another woman was on his mind. And even though Derek and his mother had a strained relationship, he cared deeply for her.

It made Ava adore him even more.

"What's going on with this job offer, Ava?" Virginia asked her as they sat on the bench in the park Ava had recreated in the venue.

"I'm supposed to be heading into Miami for a few days next week."

"So you're leaving?" Virginia didn't bother to mask the disappointment in her voice.

She didn't want to. The longer she stayed, the harder it would be to go. "I told them that I had some reservations, and they upped my salary twenty-five percent, told me I could make my own schedule and could work from home when I'm not traveling."

"How much would you be traveling?"

She was quiet for a long moment because it was too hard to think about, too hard to say. "A lot."

Out of the corner of her eye Ava saw a flash of red that made her turn around. Derek's mother had walked into the room. The dance had started more than two hours ago. Derek had already made his speech and said his thank-yous. It was an important night for him, and Anita had missed most of it. She knew that even though he hadn't directly said anything that he wanted her to be there. He wanted her to act like most mothers would when their sons pulled off such a complicated feat. Supportive. Happy for the child's success. But Anita walked into the room wearing a short, tight, red mini dress, on her arm a man that appeared to be a few years younger than Derek. It was a different man from the last one they had seen her with.

"I've got to go," she told Virginia, getting up.

"What. Why?"

"Derek's mother is here." Ava made a beeline for Anita, who had headed straight for the bar. Ava's heels and the crush of people in the room slowed her progress. As she reached Anita, she had just downed one shot and was ordering another one.

"More tequila, please!" She slammed down the shot glass on the counter. Her voice was too loud. Her words slurred just a bit. There was a bit of wildness in her eyes. The kind of look you would see in a hurt, bewildered wild animal.

"Anita." Ava tried to keep her voice bright and plastered a smile on her face. She knew that they were being watched. "How are you? We weren't sure you were coming."

"Oh, I'm here. The prick who dumped me isn't going to stop me from having a good time." She looped her arms around the neck of the man she was with. "Isn't that right, baby? Tonight you are going to make sure I have a good time."

Anita kissed the man. It was one of those overtly sexual kisses that seemed more suited for behind private doors. Something inside Ava snapped. Anita wouldn't be doing this tonight. She wouldn't allow it.

Ava didn't know how she knew Derek was behind her. But she could sense him. She turned to see that he was walking toward them, his face blank. He shut down around his mother. Every time. Without fail. It was like whatever little happiness he was experiencing she drained from him. *Not tonight.*

"Let's grab some fresh air, Anita."

"What? No. I just got here. I came here to party."

Ava grabbed her arm, and, without losing the smile on her face, she tugged Anita toward the exit.

"Hey! What do you think you're doing?"

"Lower your voice." She tightened her grip even more and kept Anita moving. Once they were in the parking lot, she let her go and swiveled to face her. Anita's date had followed them. He was little more than a kid. "You go home right this instant," she barked at him before returning her attention to Anita. "Explain yourself. You couldn't have possibly planned to ruin this night for no reason, so I'm going to need you to explain yourself."

Anita touched her chest and looked indignant. "I don't know what you're talking about."

"You know exactly what I'm talking about! Why the hell did you show up here tonight?"

"My son invited me. Contrary to what you think, I'm still the most important woman in his life."

"And I would hope he would be the most important man in yours. But you're pathetic."

"Excuse me."

"You knew how important this event was to him. He has been planning this week for months, and you show up here, stinking of wine and with a boy who looks too young to drink."

"I got dumped. I didn't want to be alone, and no one picked up the phone when I called."

"So what? You're not a child. You're entitled to feel hurt, but you're not entitled to hurt him anymore. I refuse to let you. I refuse to let you use him anymore. I refuse to allow you to drain his joy. You don't get to do this anymore. You stay the hell away from him."

"You're telling me I can't see my son? Who the hell do you think you are?"

"The woman who cares about him most in life. And if you try it with him again, I'm coming for you, and that's a promise."

"Ava!" She heard Derek's angry voice behind her. She flinched, but she ignored it.

"Get in my car, Anita. I'm taking you home."

"No. She is going to get in my car." Ava heard Nanny's voice. She turned around to see the older woman, who was absolutely furious. "I have never been more ashamed of you. I don't care how grown you are. This foolish behavior will come to an end tonight."

Anita's shoulders slumped, but she turned without a word and went to her mother's car.

That left Ava and Derek alone. "We're going home right now."

"But the party…"

"Now. Get in my car." His voice was low and a little deadly, but she obeyed him. She expected him to start yelling at her, but he remained silent their entire trip home. They walked into her house. He shut the door behind them and leaned against it. His body was tight, and tonight he somehow looked bigger than usual. He was angry. The heat rolled off him in waves.

"Did you ban my mother from seeing me?"

"I will not apologize!" she shouted at him. "She's not allowed to do this. She's not allowed to hurt you anymore. I won't let her. You can pretend it doesn't hurt, Derek, but I know it does. I don't want you hurting anymore if I can prevent it."

The look on Derek's face changed to horror, and it was then she realized that she had begun to cry.

She swiped angrily at her tears. How the hell did this happen? How did she go from hating him to crying for him? How did his happiness become more important than hers? She was doing it again. She was putting a man first, and she

had promised herself that she wasn't going to do that ever
again. She had promised herself that she was going to live
her own life, live for herself. She was taking that job. She
was moving off the island as soon as possible. He was too
much for her, too soon after such a major change in her life.

She went to walk away from him, but he grabbed her
arm and pulled her body into his. The kiss that he gave her
wasn't sweet; it wasn't gentle or comforting or loving. It
was a hot, hard kiss full of raw need. The air left her lungs,
the blood rushed out of her head and arousal had taken
over all her senses. Her mind stopped working; her body
just moved. She pulled at his tie, yanked at the buttons on
his shirt, tried to pull off his suit jacket. He pushed her
against the wall, yanked at her underwear, shredding the
fabric with his hands. It was a second later that he pushed
inside her, the hard invasion made her nearly black out.
She wrapped her leg around him as he pumped inside her
furiously in a hard pace that made her cry out and tremble
and turn to mush.

Her orgasm came on quick and hard, and Derek slammed
into her one last time before his climax took him over. They
sank to the floor, their legs unable to hold them up any
longer.

He wrapped his arm around her and pressed kisses all
over her face. "I'm confused. Are you mad at me or not?"

"I'm not mad at you," he whispered. "You're not allowed
to end this. To push me away. To try to have space from
me. I need you."

She nodded and then kissed him. She needed him, too.

# Chapter 19

Derek's office had changed a lot in the past month. It was now *his* office. Nothing remained from the former mayor. No more bulky, overpriced furniture. No tacky gold walls. His handmade furniture was there, his bookshelves. He spent more time in here than he ever had, and that was Ava's fault. He never thought he would be here more than once a week, but he couldn't get any work done at home, because home was where he spent time with Ava. If he worked there, he was more likely to work longer hours and let his worlds meld. Over the past few months he had discovered that while this island and its people were a huge part of his life, it wasn't his entire life. He spent his mornings in his shop, his afternoons here, but when five o'clock came, everything stopped and he went home to her.

Life was better that way. Except for this week, because Ava had been gone. She had been in Miami for the past three days in a sort of training for her new job. He had been through some pretty dark times but this had been the hardest three days of his life. He felt empty. Even though they FaceTimed every night, it wasn't enough. She was his home and without her he felt directionless. It made him think about the future. His term was up at the end of the year, just four more months, even less time before the election. He hadn't campaigned the last two times because no one ran against him. But maybe it was time to give this up. He could be proud of what he had accomplished. There would be other ways to fill up his time, to work for the greater good. There wouldn't be another Ava.

"Hello, son."

Derek was surprised to see his father standing just inside his office door. They were supposed to meet for lunch, but they hadn't gotten their schedules to line up yet, still Derek thought he would be heading to Miami to meet his father. He didn't think the man would step foot on this island again, but here he was in his office. Such a change from when he was a kid and he walked into his father's huge office, seeing the man who he looked so much like appearing large and intimidating behind his desk.

"Dad, what are you doing here?"

"Came to see my boy. Heard you had open office hours on Thursdays. Figured this was the best way to get some face time with you."

"Have a seat, Dad. I must admit that I find it a little satisfying to be sitting on the other side of the desk. I have all the power here. I could have you thrown in jail for three years and you couldn't stop me."

"You want to have me thrown in jail?" He raised a brow as he took a seat.

"I don't," Derek answered honestly. "How have you been since we last spoke?"

"Fine. I'm more concerned about you. If you're going to declare your candidacy for Senate, we'll have to start preparing."

"I'm not going to run. I'm not sure I'll be mayor of this town next year."

"Why?"

"It might be time to let someone else have it."

"Does this have anything to do with Ava?"

"She didn't ask me to give it up if that's what you're asking."

"But she asked you to give your mother up?"

Derek froze for a moment. "No. Have you spoken to Mom?"

"She called me. I picked up. We talked about you."

"I don't want to have this conversation. My entire life I've been in the middle of this strange dance you two have going on. Do you know what it's like to be raised by someone who hates you as much as they love you? Every important event that I have ever had she has messed up or in some way made it about her. I was furious when she showed up at the founder's day dance drunk and all over some frat boy. Ava just did what I didn't have the guts to do. She held her accountable. Ava can't ban me from seeing my mother, but I can say no more and put some distance between us."

"She said you've been putting distance between you two ever since Ava came into the picture."

Derek shook his head. "And you believed her?"

"She's threatened by Ava. Ava is a tough thing and your mother isn't. I think she's afraid that she's going to lose what little relationship she has left with you if you continue on with this girl."

"I am continuing on. And I tried with Mom, but I'm done now. It's her turn to try, and you can tell her that. I'm tired."

Victor nodded. "You should talk to your mother. Really talk to her. I think you'll understand her a little better or at least understand why I fell in love with her so hard."

Derek nodded. "One day."

"Don't wait too long." He stood up. "I don't want to take

up too much of your time, but I would love to have dinner with you and your lovely girlfriend soon. I've missed this island. I think I'll be coming back here more."

His father walked out before Derek could wrap his head around what had just happened.

His parents were speaking again. He didn't know what was going to happen between them, but he was sure he wasn't going to get in the middle of it. If there was one thing he'd learned in these past few months it was that sometimes he just had to worry about his own happiness.

"Excuse me, Mr. Mayor, are you busy?" His happiness had just walked through the door.

He stood up, surprised and unbelievably happy to see her. "I thought you weren't supposed to be back for another two days."

"I came home early." She dropped her bag and rushed toward him. "I missed you."

He wrapped his arms around her and hugged her tightly to him. How did he go without this feeling for so long? "I thought you were heading to New York last night. You were at the airport when we last spoke. Did things go poorly?"

"No. They went really, really well. Everyone is incredibly nice and beautiful and they all have great clothes. It's a great company to work for."

"But…"

"I kept thinking I wish I had never met you."

"Ouch."

"It's a compliment. I couldn't concentrate. I kept thinking about you and what you were doing and how long it would be till I could speak to you again. How am I supposed to be my own person when every thought and action is tied up in you?"

A tear slid down her face, and he caught it with his thumb. "I don't know. It's something you're going to have to figure out because you're not allowed to end this, remember?"

"I know. I'm not ending this."

*Yet.* He was expecting her to say yet, but it hadn't come.

Ava sat on the sand, watching the waves violently crash against the shore. The wind had kicked up in the last hour, blowing her hair and dress wildly, but she couldn't force herself to move. This tiny beach just down the road from her house was like paradise for her. Even with a storm moving closer to the island, she still found it peaceful. She could think here, think about how much her life had changed since she'd come here in April. It was early September now, and she hadn't planned to be on the island this long. But a few weeks had turned into a few months, and her annoying next-door neighbor somehow turned into the love of her life. She went from being unemployed to having a dream job fall into her lap. This should be the happiest time in her life, but she was feeling so damn confused. She didn't trust her instincts anymore. She didn't know what was right.

She hadn't realized that her entire family hated the man she was going to marry. She had no clue he had been splitting his time with his other family. She had given up everything for a man who didn't really love her, and she had been blindsided when it all came crashing down. What if that happened to her with Derek? What if she were missing the signs again? She couldn't take another heartbreak. She had been trying to keep her distance because she knew that this time would be worse. But she had failed miserably and only ended up loving him more.

"Ava?"

Derek sat down beside her on the beach. "I thought I would find you here. I was worried about you." She looked up at him. He was in a green hooded sweatshirt and in his hand was a sweatshirt for her. "Put this on. It's getting cold."

The gesture made her smile. It was one of his sweatshirts. He could have grabbed one of her jackets, but he knew she liked this sweatshirt of his. She liked the way it smelled like him. She liked putting something on her body that had been pressed against his. He was so thoughtful, always. He didn't give her big, lavish gifts, but it was the small things. Picking up her favorite ice cream when he left work, sitting through romantic comedies that must have bored him to tears, bringing her trinkets he'd seen in stores that made him think of her. A high-heeled-shoe key chain, a pen with a fire design, one of those paperweights in the shape of a diamond ring. He joked that no one would be able to give her a bigger ring than him.

He loved her. He must, right? Only he hadn't said it. Not once. He hadn't asked her not to take the job. He had only been supportive. He had even bought her a brand-new designer briefcase when she had gone to Miami.

She wanted him to ask her not to go. She wanted to hear that he loved her. She wanted to hear that he wanted to make his home on the island with her and he wouldn't settle for anything else. But he was leaving it completely up to her. Maybe because he was unsure of them. Unsure they could make a life together.

He wouldn't pressure her for it, and that made her hate him a little, but it also made her love him even more. The only one she could blame for her decision was herself, so it had to be the right one or she would never forgive herself.

"You always know where to find me. It makes it damn hard to hide from you."

"That's because I put a tracking chip inside your arm one night while you were sleeping."

"Did you?" She laughed. "I thought that was a rather large mosquito bite."

"Are you really trying to hide from me?"

"Not for long. The sex is too good." She leaned against him, and for a moment they were both quiet as they stared at the ocean. "It's beautiful, isn't it?"

"Yes, but we can't sit here much longer."

"Stupid hurricanes ruining my navel-gazing."

"I want you to pack a bag. I'm going to take you to the other side of the island to your brother's house. His house is built to withhold a storm this size."

Storms had made her uneasy her entire life, and this one was projected to be the biggest one the island had seen in years. Rationally she knew that being with her family at her brother's home was the best place she could be, but she didn't want to be there without Derek. He was her safe place.

"Where are you going to be?"

"I'm the head of the emergency response team. Part of our job is to prepare the island before a disaster strikes so that lives are saved. I'm going to be evacuating the houses that are in the direct path of the storm and helping our citizens board up the businesses on the waterfront. Then I'm going to be at the community center all night. That's where most of the evacuated families will be staying."

"And you are planning to stick me at my brother's house?"

"Yes. This is more than just thundershowers. It's a hurricane. I need you someplace safe." As soon as he said the words, the first drops of rain hit them. "I won't be able to work unless I know you are." He stood up and pulled her to her feet.

"I can help prepare for the storm. I want to."

"Ava." He shut his eyes briefly. "Please. Just go to your brother's house. I need you to do this for me."

"And I won't be able to think about anything else all

night if I know you are out there combing the streets for
foolish people and runaway animals."

"I won't be."

"I won't be going to my brother's house, either. I'll pack
a bag, but I'm going with you and you can't stop me."

He couldn't stop her from coming with him. She had
been by his side the entire day as the storm grew closer
and the wind started to tear apart the island. He knew she
was terrified of storms. It was wrong of him, but he liked
when there was a storm, when she would sleep so close to
him, her body wrapped tightly around his, her nose buried in his neck. But today, even though he could see her
discomfort, she was a force to be reckoned with. Ava had
incredible organization skills. She could get people to mo-
bilize in a way that he couldn't.

She had gotten teenagers to help, young men and women
who were quick and strong and by 3:00 p.m. they had
boarded up fifteen restaurants and homes. By five, when
the storm was dumping buckets of water down on them
and the waves were eating away at the sand on the beach,
they had evacuated most of the families who lived on the
water and gotten everyone to safety.

Ava had card games going and bingo that night at the
center. She had designated a room for movies and a quiet
room just for reading or conversations. His grandmother,
cousin and aunts had come, even though their homes
weren't on the evacuation route and they had cooked large
vats of soups and made more than a hundred sandwiches.
It was almost like a party, designed by Ava to keep their
minds off the destruction happening outside. Derek was
very aware, though. Most of the windows had been covered
in the front of the building where everyone was gathered
but not in the back of the building. Every half hour or so
he slipped away to look outside. He could barely see, only

sheets of water and trees that were being violently pulled by the strong winds. Every once in a while he would see an object pass by the window, a picnic table, a bicycle. Objects heavy enough to cause major damage to a lot of property. He was worried about his little island, terrified for the devastation that might be caused.

This storm had come out of nowhere. They were as prepared as they could be. But this was one of those things where the outcome was completely unpredictable. And Derek knew that one major storm could decimate this island, the recovery could cost millions, their economy would be devastated.

He felt arms wrap around him, and for a split second he thought they might be Ava's, but they didn't feel right. He would know Ava's touch anywhere.

He looked down to see his mother, in sweats and rain boots, her hair up in a bun, looking quite unlike herself. "What are you doing here? Your house is in the center of the island. You didn't have to evacuate."

"I know, but my entire family is here, and I'm tired of feeling left out."

"Excuse me?" He stepped away from her touch. "You feel left out? You left yourself out. For years. Birthdays, holidays. My graduation. You weren't even there when I got sworn in for mayor and I'm supposed to feel sorry for you? Stop playing the victim all the time. If you feel left out, maybe you need to jog your memory and remember exactly where you were for the past thirty years."

"When you let me have it, you really let me have it. Don't you?"

"I've got more to say. I'm angry with you."

"You should be."

"You were a better girlfriend than you ever were a mother, and if it weren't for Aunt Clara and Uncle Hal, I'm not sure where I would be."

"I'm grateful for them every day."

"Stop it! I'm trying to yell at you, and you keep agreeing with me."

"I know." She shook her head. "I've been a bad mother to you. Don't you think I know that? Don't you think I have seen how much I have disappointed you over the years? I was nineteen when I had you. I didn't know how to be a mother. Or a wife, or even a good friend. But I had you, and I chased after your father like a crazy person for all those years."

Derek found a chair and sat down heavily on it. His mother sounded sensible and rational. She didn't sound like herself at all. "If you knew all of this, why did you continue to behave that way? Why do you still continue to behave this way?"

"I'm broken. I was eighteen and beautiful and full of promise. I had a full scholarship for dance at one of the best schools in the country and then a bad car accident took all of that away from me in a moment. I couldn't dance anymore. I could no longer sit through classes in college. I was too scattered to hold down a regular job. I felt like less than nothing, and then when your father came along, I focused all of my attention on loving him. Because he made me feel worthy. And then you came along, and I thought I would finally be set. That we would be this perfect little family. But nothing worked out that way, and I was left with a man who didn't really love me and a kid I didn't know how to mother. I love you, Derek. You're the best part of me, but Lord knows I don't understand you. I never have. It was so easy for my sisters. They just looked at you, and you loved them. I knew you needed more of them in your lives and less of me."

"I wanted you. You were my mother. You made me feel like you didn't want me."

"Of course I wanted you! Your aunt and uncle asked for

you a thousand times, but I just couldn't do it. I couldn't give you up. But I didn't know how to be your mother, either. I know I was selfish, and when I stayed away, it's not because I wanted to be away, it's because I thought you were better off without me. It's because I knew I embarrassed you. I knew I could never be the type of mother you needed. And that's why I always keep this distance between us. I can take you rejecting the vapid me, or the scattered me, or the hot mess me. But I can't take you rejecting the me who tries and just can't live up."

"Damn it, Mom." He didn't know what to say. How to process it all. "I wouldn't reject you."

"I've been trying for years to get you to. I've been waiting for you to tell me off and cut me out of your life for good, but you've never done it. Even when I have really deserved it. You're annoyingly moral and kind, and it's really hard to be the parent to someone who is so much better than you."

The corner of his mouth curled into a smile. "Ava says I'm annoyingly moral, too."

"Ah, Ava. The little drill sergeant. I hate her."

"She's incredible."

"That's the reason why I hate her. She's the kind of person I wanted so desperately to be. Beautiful, smart, talented. She snagged a billionaire and then dumped *him*! And she takes care of your heart. She loves you. She makes you smile. You'd be an idiot to let her go."

"I'm not planning to." He still didn't know how she felt. Sometimes he felt like she had one foot out the door; the other half of her he was sure wanted to stay forever. All he knew for sure was that she hadn't turned down the job offer yet. More and more phone calls had been exchanged. There was mention of spending next spring in New York. None of it was a good sign for them, and yet he was determined not to let her go. He would leave this island, leave the people he loved behind for her.

She had been asked to give up everything for a man before, but now it was time for a man to give everything up for her.

# Chapter 20

Nearly everyone was asleep, and Ava was surprised by how silent one room could be with dozens of people in it. The only thing she heard was the howling of the wind. She knew she should go to sleep, too, but she couldn't. There was too much on her mind. She had seen Derek's mother follow him to the back of the building a couple of hours ago. Neither one of them had been seen since. Her first instinct was to go, to protect him from Anita, but she knew she was being foolish. Derek could handle himself. He was a strong man, and, despite everything, he loved his mother. He would honor her. He would try to work things out instead of cutting her out of his life. He would do what good men did.

"Ava." She felt a touch on her shoulder as she heard his voice. "Come," he whispered as he took her hand and led her to a small office on the far side of the building. He had turned it into a bedroom. There was an air mattress on the floor, a thick homemade blanket, a small portable television. There was even soup and bread left over from dinner. She realized that she had served people all night, but she hadn't eaten anything herself.

"This is the best thing I have seen all day," she said, squeezing his hand.

"I aim to please, ma'am. Even during a hurricane."

"How are you doing, Mr. Mayor?" She wrapped her arms around him. She knew that when he slipped away he was listening to weather reports, looking out the uncovered windows, trying to predict the damage to his beloved island.

"Worried, but by the sound of the reports, the worst of it is over. Sit down. Eat. You've been on your feet all day."

"So have you," she pointed out. "Sit with me."

He nodded, and they both eased down on the air mattress. "You should eat." He stroked his hand down her back. "I don't think you have since breakfast."

"I'm not hungry right now." Holding him close was filling her up. "You were with your mother for a long time. Did you have a good talk?"

"Yes. I'm not sure if things will ever be good between my mother and me, but I know they will be okay. I think I understand her a little more."

"She's going to try harder?"

"Yes, I told her you'll beat her up if she doesn't."

"I will." They were quiet for a long moment. "I love you, Derek."

"What?" He pulled away from her slightly and frowned. She hadn't meant to tell him then, even though she had been feeling it for months. Still she expected a different reaction from him, a smile. Something more.

"I'm in love with you," she said, unable to stop herself. "I've known it for a while now. I've been trying to think back to the exact moment it happened, but I can't. I just knew that one day I woke up in love like I have never been in love before. Like I didn't think was possible. I can't see living my life without you in it. I want you to be the father of my children. I want to go to bed every night beside you. I want to grow old with you. You're my home."

"What about your job?"

"Do you want to know what I was thinking about on the beach?"

He shook his head.

"There's a shop two doors down from your storefront that's vacant. I was thinking about opening my own boutique. There are a lot of seniors on the island that would love to work, and there are teenagers that could use some job experience. We could do some mentoring there. There's a lot of possibilities. I could be my own boss and…" She trailed off, realizing that she was starting to ramble. None of these thoughts were fully formed. This morning she was still unsure what she was going to do about the job, but deep in her heart she knew she couldn't leave Derek. She couldn't leave this island.

There was so much love here. The entire town came out to board up businesses and save people's homes. There was no place on earth that could compare with this. And there was no other man. He was good for her. He made life better. How could she risk that for a job?

"Say something."

He opened his mouth to speak when a large crash reverberated through the building. He looked at her, into her eyes, before he shook his head and rushed out of the room without a word. Not a smile. Not a squeeze of her hand. Not a single clue that he was feeling what she was feeling. She had been so sure that he loved her.

Derek rushed toward the sound of the crash. He feared the worst, some sort of heavy object crashing through a window and injuring the people in the room. But he was relieved to see that the kitchen door had been forced open by the wind and smacked against the wall so hard that a shelf collapsed, knocking all the pots and pans to the floor. One of the police officers present sprang up when he heard the crash and together they pushed the heavy door closed again. The wind was still wild and howling, but the rain seemed to have slowed down substantially. Wind damage was bad, but it was the flooding Derek was more concerned with. Broken windows could be fixed. Extreme flooding would mean so many more problems.

"Thanks, Mike," he said to the officer. "Would you mind calming everyone down for me? I'll clean up in here."

"I'm on it."

"Is everything okay?" Nanny walked into the kitchen. She somehow managed to look elegant in the middle of a hurricane in her heather-gray cashmere loungewear.

"Yeah, just a runaway door. Everything is under control now."

"You're smiling."

"Am I?"

"I guess you don't need a reason to smile after closing the door that just scared the spit out of all of us, but one does wonder why you look so ridiculously happy right now."

"She loves me."

"Ava? Yes, dear. Anyone who has seen the way she looks at you knows that."

"She told me she loves me. She told me she wants to make a life with me. Here on this island. We're going to raise our family here." He realized that he had left her alone in the room without responding to her earth-shattering statement. "I have to go back to her. I have to ask her to marry me." He turned to go to her.

"Wait! You need a ring." She slipped her beloved ring from her finger and handed it to him. "This is meant to be on her finger now."

He looked at the ring that he knew Ava had loved and

felt a moment of apprehension. The ring had rested on his grandmother's finger his entire life. There were times, when he was a boy, that he caught his grandfather touching it as he stroked her hand, pride in his eyes. It seemed wrong to take it from her. It seemed like it was breaking the connection she felt with her husband who was no longer here. "I'm not sure I can accept this."

"You don't have a choice. This has been passed down through the males in our family for a century. If I don't give this to you, his mother will haunt me for the rest of my life. And believe me—that woman could nag. I want Ava to have this ring. I knew the moment I met her that this would be hers one day. Besides, your grandfather was a very smart man. He got me a replacement one twenty years ago. I'm just glad I finally get to wear it."

"Thank you." He let out a breath. "This is perfect."

"Go on. Go ask her. We're going to need a reason to celebrate once this terrible storm is over."

He nodded and took off toward Ava, but when he got back to the room where he'd left her, she wasn't there.

In fact, she was nowhere to be found.

It was much harder to hide in the daylight. People in the community center were up early the next morning eager to see the damage that had been done to their homes and businesses. So when the first police officers went outside to assess the roads and damage, Ava slipped out, too. She couldn't be around all those people. She couldn't look anyone in the eye. She didn't want to see Derek's family, who were all there that night, because they would take one look at her and just know.

He had been gone for a long time last night, and for a while she waited, expecting him to come back and say something to her. Max was full of fake I-love-yous, but she knew Derek was the type of man who only said it when he meant it, and he hadn't said it yet. He hadn't said it to her once. She knew there had been no broken windows last night. The loud bang was just from a door that blew open. He must be thinking about what he was going to say to her. Something like: "I care deeply for you, but I'm just not ready to get that serious."

She had probably scared him off. She couldn't leave it at I love you. She had to tell him that she wanted to grow old with him, that she wanted to carry his children. He was a man who had never been committed to anyone. That should have tipped her off, given her the first clue that maybe it was because he didn't want to be.

She stepped out on the street in front of the community center. Things didn't look too bad. There were kids' toys and patio furniture on the ground. Trash cans that escaped from their homes. A few cars had cracked windshields. Others seemed perfectly fine. As far as she could see, no trees had been uprooted, no power lines knocked down.

She might be able to walk home. The walk was just a bit more than a mile. She thought about calling her brother to get her, or maybe catching a ride with one of the people leaving this morning.

"Where the hell have you been?" Derek grabbed her shoulder and spun her around to face him. He was furious. More angry than she had ever seen him. His nostrils were flared, his body was tight, his eyes full of fire. She tried to back away from him, but he grabbed her shoulders, preventing her flight. "Do you have any idea how worried I was?" he roared at her. "I looked for you all night. I thought you did something stupid and walked home in the middle of a hurricane. I called your cell phone a hundred times."

"I'm not stupid enough to walk home in a hurricane."

"Why did you leave?"

"Why do you think I left? Because I didn't want to see you!"

"Why not?"

"Why not? Why not! I tell you that I love you. I spill my guts to you, and you say nothing. Not a damn thing. Do you know how hard it was for me to trust again? Do you know how stupid I feel for falling in love with another man who doesn't love me back?"

"Are you insane? Have you lost your mind? Seriously, Ava. You are spoiled. You are used to getting what you want when you want it. My town was being hit with the largest storm we have ever seen. There was a loud explosion. I've got a hundred people here that I'm accountable for, so excuse me if I needed to go make sure no one was being crushed while we were sharing a tender moment."

"No one was being crushed. It was a damn door! You were stalling for time, trying to figure out a way to let me down easy."

"I can't believe this is the woman you sent me!" he said to the sky. He grabbed her hand and pulled her back inside. The building was full of people milling about; the smell of pancakes had begun to waft through the air. "Excuse me, everyone. Can I please have your attention?"

"What the hell are you doing, Derek?"

"Proving a point." He looked back to the crowd, which had suddenly gone silent. "I'm afraid that this woman standing next to me doesn't realize that I'm in love with her."

"Of course you're in love with her," someone said from the crowd.

"Thank you," Derek responded. "This woman challenges me. She gets under my skin. She makes me want to pull my hair out."

"You're no day at the beach yourself," she retorted.

"But I love her," Derek said firmly. "I'm insanely in love with her. So much so that I was and am willing to give up living on this island and being your mayor to be with her."

"What!" Ava said as she heard groans of dismay. "You are not leaving this island. I wouldn't let you."

"You wouldn't have a choice. If you leave, I will follow you. If you take a job halfway across the world, I will be there to hold your passport. You were meant for me, Ava, and there is nothing in this world I wouldn't do to be with you."

"I would never ask you to leave your home, you idiot." Her eyes filled with tears.

"And I would never ask you to give up a dream job to be with me."

"I'm not giving it up for you. I'm giving it up for myself because my life would be too empty without you in it every day."

He got down on one knee. "Finally, we agree on something." He pulled a ring out of his pocket. His grandmother's ring. The one she had admired so much. "I want you to be the mother of my children. I want to grow old with you. I want to wake up every day for the rest of my life beside you. So, I'm asking you in front of the entire town to be my wife. Will you marry me?"

She was stunned silent. All she could do was look at him, her eyes so filled with tears that she could barely see him.

"For God's sake, Ava, put the man out of his misery and say yes." She turned at the sound of her twin's voice. He was standing just behind her; in fact, her entire family was standing behind her.

"How?" she asked Derek.

"I called them when I couldn't find you this morning. They came right down. Now, can I have my answer, please?"

"Yes!" She collapsed on him. "Yes, yes. Of course yes. Yes."

"Good." He exhaled. And when he kissed her, there wasn't a dry eye in the house.

* * * * *

*A game of seduction*

Pamela Yaye

*Seduced*
BY THE BACHELOR

Tatiyana Washington will do whatever it takes to right a wrong for her sister—even if it means deceiving one of LA's most celebrated attorneys. Once Markos Morretti discovers they have met under false pretenses, he desires her even more. Faced with a decision, will he choose the promise of love?

**The Morretti Millionaires**

*Available March 2017!*

www.Harlequin.com

KPPY489

# Get 2 Free Books,
## Plus 2 Free Gifts—
### just for trying the Reader Service!

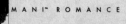

# SPECIAL EXCERPT FROM

## ◈ HARLEQUIN®

KIMANI
ROMANCE

*An ambitious daughter of a close-knit Louisiana clan,
Kamaya Boudreaux is making a name for herself in the
business world. But when her secret venture is threatened
to be exposed, she needs to do some serious damage
control. Her plans don't include giving in to temptation
with her sexy business partner, Wesley Walters...*

*Read on for a sneak peek at
A PLEASING TEMPTATION, the next exciting
installment in author Deborah Fletcher Mello's
THE BOUDREAUX FAMILY series!*

Wesley reached into the briefcase that rested beside his
chair leg. He passed her the folder of documents. "They're
all signed," he said as he extended his hand to shake hers.
"I look forward to working with you, Kamaya Boudreaux."

She slid her palm against his, the warmth of his touch
heating her spirit. "Same here, Wesley Walters. I imagine
we're going to make a formidable team."

"Team! I like that."

"You should. Because it's so out of character for me! I
don't usually play well with others."

He chuckled. "Then I'm glad you chose me to play
with first."

KPEXP0317

A cup of coffee and a few questions kept Kamaya and Wesley talking for almost three hours. After sharing more than either had planned, they stood, saying their goodbyes and making plans to see each other again.

"I would really love to take you to dinner," Wesley said as he walked Kamaya to her car.

"Are you asking me out on a date, Wesley Walters?"

He grinned. "I am. With one condition."

"What's that?"

"We don't talk business. I get the impression that's not an easy thing for you to do. So will you accept the challenge?"

As they reached her car, she smiled as she nodded her head. "I'd love to."

"I mean it about not talking business."

Kamaya laughed. "You really don't know me."

He laughed with her. "I don't, but I definitely look forward to changing that."

Wesley opened the door of her vehicle. The air between them was thick and heavy, carnal energy sweeping from one to the other, fervent with desire. It was intense and unexpected, and left them both feeling a little awkward and definitely excited about what might come.

"Drive safely, Kamaya," he whispered softly, watching as she slid into the driver's seat.

She nodded. "You, too, Wesley. Have a really good night."

*Don't miss A PLEASING TEMPTATION*
*by Deborah Fletcher Mello, available April 2017*
*wherever Harlequin® Kimani Romance™*
*books and ebooks are sold.*